I0538704

THE TWISTED MIND OF
CLETUS COMPTON

SUSAN KEENE

Other Publications by Susan Keene

Finding Lizzy Smith (Kate Nash 1)
Who's Roxy Watkins? (Kate Nash 2)
Tattered Wings

Published by
Bent Willow Books

ISBN-10: 0-9898831-3-2
ISBN-13: 978-0-9898831-3-9

DEDICATED

to

Blenna, without whose support this would not be possible.

ACKNOWLEDGMENTS

A special thanks to all first responders, EMTs, paramedics, firefighters, and law officers who put their lives on the line daily to protect us from people like the Compton brothers.

Thanks to Webster County Sheriff Roye Cole for his technical help; Tierney James who is always there to pump me up with words of encouragement, to Wanda Fittro, Lois Curran, and Linda K Freeman who lent their support and to Sharon Kizziah-Holmes who always goes above and beyond.

CHAPTER ONE

"Dean! Stop! Did you see that?" Dr. Boo Jordan put her hand on her husband's arm.

Dean Jordan stopped with such force his wife lurched forward and had to put her hand on the dashboard to keep from slamming into it. "No, I didn't see anything. What was it?"

"I'm not sure. Can you back up?" She turned in her seat as far as she could to try to look back at the road behind her.

"Sure, but this isn't the ideal time or place for exploring. I can hardly see the road the fog is so thick."

"Something is alive back there," Boo said.

"Probably a raccoon or possum, but I'll turn around and shine the lights on whatever you saw." Dean maneuvered the car around on the narrow farm road. It took several tries. They were in Boo's

SUV, the large vehicle wheels made the task more daunting. He went forward and back several times, until his headlights shined on his wife's area of concern.

"There it is," she said. "My flashlight is under your seat. Can you get it? I hate to leave something in distress out here for the coyotes to eat."

"Okay, but you stay here. No use for both of us to get wet and muddy." Dean, always the gentleman.

Boo chuckled. "I might be retired, but I'm still a trained FBI agent."

"I know. If I need back up, I'll call out." She took it as a compliment.

Boo opened her door and swung her feet out of the car and onto to the ground. The fog hung like Spanish moss, thick and an eerie green in the flat beam of the lights.

Most likely, it would turn out to be puppies. For some reason, people loved to drop unwanted pets in the country. Boo and Dean had a wonderful dog they rescued from a box on this road.

"Can we agree if it's puppies, we don't keep them?" Dean shinned the light in front of him and walked toward a wooden crate about ten feet off the road.

Boo didn't answer.

She watched as Dean's shadowy figure approached the crate. He took another step and became a ghostly shadow in the fog. She followed the muted glow of the light as it moved from place to place.

The fog got heavier by the moment. A fine

drizzle covered everything, as a cold front swept through the area. Boo strained to see. She stood and took a couple of steps toward where Dean disappeared. He came out of the fog so close to her she stepped back. "Is that a child?"

"Yes. A girl I think. It's hard to tell."

"Oh, my goodness. What's that on her wrist?"

Dean raised the child's arm for her to see. "Looks like a crude handcuff of some sort. I'm torn between calling the sheriff and taking her home."

"I'm for taking her home. We can call Tony later." Boo reached for the girl. She felt so light. Her hair clung to her head. She smelled like a mixture of dirt, grime and something akin to horse feed and urine.

"You're going to ruin your clothes. Do you still have a blanket in the back? I'll wrap her. She's shivering."

"This coat isn't important." Boo would never put a material possession ahead of a human need.

Dean Jordan handed the girl to his wife, got the blanket, and came back to tuck it around the waif his wife now held tight to her chest. The girl made the first sound they had heard from her. "Thank you," she said in a quiet but clear voice.

Boo felt the girl relax on the ride home.

The Jordans had a farm about four miles south from where they found her. Dean turned the heater on high and focused his attention on the road. The dense fog enveloped them. The added drizzle caused a glare where the headlights hit the road. "I hope there are no more kids out there." Boo held the girl and rubbed a warm hand up and down her back, through the wrap.

"No, I'm the only one, right now."

"What do you mean, right now?" Dean asked.

"Let's talk later," Boo shook her head at Dean. "I'm sure our little friend is hungry and cold."

The girl remained silent and still. Boo's heart bled, thinking about how a child got into a situation like this.

When they arrived at the farm, Dean pulled the car close to the porch. The drizzle became a downpour as they ran into the house. September weather in the Ozarks could change daily. The last few days were in the low seventies. The temperature, tonight, would drop into the thirties as a cold front raced through the area. Outside was no place for a child, or anyone else for that matter.

"Are you hungry?" Boo asked.

"Yes." The mention of food perked her up. Dean fixed a peanut butter and jelly sandwich and a glass of milk and set it in front of her.

Boo went upstairs to find the smallest clothes she could to put on the girl. The ones she wore where dripping wet.

She found a pair of sweat pants and a tee shirt she could sacrifice. With the legs cut shorter and the top tied in the right places, they would serve the purpose. At the bottom of the stairs, Boo stopped and listened to the conversation in the kitchen.

"What's your name?"

"Courtney Sue Hamilton, I live at 9217 Chambers Lane in Davenport, Iowa. My phone number is 555-821-1734. I am 6 years old. My birthday is September 19."

"That's awesome, Courtney, did your Mom teach you that?"

"No, my teacher, Mrs. James. She said I might need to know it one day."

Boo took the opportunity to step into the kitchen. "I couldn't help but overhear your conversation. Let's get you out of those wet clothes and into something dry. Your birthday is only five days away. I would like to see you celebrate it with your family. Do you have brothers and sisters?"

"I have twin brothers, Dallas and Dalton, they are four." Tears streamed down her face. "If my birthday is in five days, my brothers are already five. My sister Marcy's birthday is in November. She's nine."

Boo walked over to sit beside the child. "It's okay to cry. You've been through a lot. I'm sure the sheriff will call your parents when he gets here."

"On the mountain, you couldn't cry. The redheaded man would add time to your stay if you complained or cried. I put my blankets over my head and cried all night. When he was around, I tried to act happy and smile so I could go home sooner."

"It must have been horrible." Boo stood and opened her arms to Courtney who stepped into them. Boo turned to Dean. Could you get a pair of gloves out of the garage, and put Courtney's clothes and the chain you cut off her wrist into a plastic trash bag?"

Boo took the girl into the downstairs bathroom and helped her wash the grime off her face. She knew better than to give her a bath and perhaps wash away any clue she had on her body or in her hair.

"I am a doctor," Boo told her. "A psychiatrist. A doctor who takes care of people's minds. I would like to ask you about how you happened to end up on Bear Road, but I don't want you to have to go through it more than you have too. The sheriff is on his way. We can wait for him. He is a nice man named Tony."

As if on cue, the back doorbell rang. Dean let him in. Boo hadn't told the sheriff much. Only that they found something on the side of the road and it needed attention and couldn't wait until morning.

She wanted him to come alone. A large police presence would not be helpful to the girl at this point it might frighten her even more.

Tony Massey stood six feet six. He automatically bent his head to walk through the doorway. When he saw the girl, he looked from Dean to Boo. "Is this what you found by the side of the road?"

"Yes." Boo invited him to join them at the table and introduced the two. He took a notebook out of the breast pocket of his shirt. Boo had a legal pad in front of her. They both began taking notes.

Over the next hour, Courtney told them a fantastic story. It sounded like a plot for a novel, a scary novel.

"Mom and I were shopping at the mall with the twins. She stopped to tell them something but I kept walking." She started, "I crossed over to the other side of the hall to look in a window. A man picked me up and walked out the door. He threw me in the trunk of a car. When I got out of the trunk, I saw mountains and forest."

"Do you know the man's name?"

"No, but I will never forget what he looks like." Courtney shook her head. "Actually, there were three men on the mountain."

"Can you tell me a little about them?" Tony softened his voice.

"A redheaded man with a ponytail told us what to do. He brought new kids and took old kids away."

"Was he a big man?" Boo asked

"Not as tall as you." She pointed at Tony. "But taller than you." She pointed toward Dean.

"I want you to tell me what you remember about the other men, and life on the mountain. But before that, we have one more question." Tony looked at Boo and nodded.

Boo asked. "Did any of the men hurt you?"

"Yes and no. They made my stomach hurt when they fed me, but I ate anyway because if I refused, he called me ungrateful and didn't feed me anything the next day. My wrist hurt from the chain that kept me close to the box and my arms and legs hurt when it got so cold at night and I only had a sweatshirt for a blanket."

Boo persisted. "That's horrible, Courtney. Did they ever touch your body, ask you to touch their bodies or ask you to do anything that made you uncomfortable?"

"No. They were just mean. They never touched us at all. "

"Okay, go on with your story."

"There isn't much else to tell. A fat boy named Boyd, who lives with the two men, picks out a wooden box and chains you to it. It's outside with the bugs and animals. The other man looked funny, like somebody tried to paint him white, but it faded off. His hair, skin and eyelashes were white. Not white like us. I mean pale, like a ghost. He wore sunglasses a lot and when he took them off, he looked scary. Around his eyes he was pink."

Boo wrote albino on her pad and underlined it twice.

"We did the same thing day after day," Courtney continued. "Except sometimes when the redheaded man went to get another kid, the white guy would let us out, one at a time, to go for a walk or play in the creek. And he would feed us oranges and carrots." Courtney yawned and rubbed her eyes.

"That's enough for now." Tony looked at his watch and motioned for Boo to go into the hall with him. "It's almost midnight. She is tired and flustered. I say we give this up for the night. What do you think?"

Boo glanced back over her shoulder where the girl slumped half asleep next to Dean, who sat and patted her arm. "I think it's a great idea. Want us to keep her here?"

"It would be good, but I need to do this by the book. I will call my emergency foster mother, Thelma Freeman. I want to keep this girl a secret as long as I can. I don't want anyone to come after her."

"I agree. We don't know who abandoned her, or why. Someone might come back for her. The FBI will head this case because it's a kidnapping. I would call them before I notified her parents. There are protocols to be followed in ransom abduction cases." Boo told him.

Tony called Thelma. While they waited for her to arrive, Dean drove with the sheriff over to the place where they found the girl. They took the farm truck so they could bring the box back to the farm. Tony might need it later as evidence. If he left it near the road too long, someone would surely mess with it.

Thelma arrived before the men returned, came in and introduced herself. She smiled at Boo and went straight to the child. "Hi, Courtney, I'm Thelma. I am going to take you home with me so you can get some rest. First, we need to make a stop by the hospital to make sure you are healthy after your stay on the mountain. Do you like Teddy bears or dolls?" Thelma had four or five dolls and two teddy bears in a tote bag slung over her shoulder.

Courtney reached for a doll with dark hair and soft skin. "I have a doll like this at home." She began to cry again.

"Now, now, honey." Thelma stepped toward the girl and spoke in a soothing voice. "Let's go now. The sooner we get you checked out, the closer you are to seeing Mom and Dad."

Courtney reached up with her skinny scratched arm. Thelma took her hand. They were half way to the car when the little girl ran back to hug Boo. "Thank you."

"I am glad we could help." She kissed the top of the child's head.

"Tell Tony we are going straight to Moxie Hospital. He can meet us there," Thelma said as they were leaving.

Boo shook her head yes, then crossed her arms over her chest to protect herself from the cold. She stood on the porch and stared at the car as it disappeared into the darkness and fog. She heard their truck bouncing down the driveway and went in to make coffee.

CHAPTER TWO

Cletus Compton sat on his front porch. He called it a porch, but no one else would describe it as such. An array of wooden pallets lay on bare ground, held together with sticks, rocks, and pieces of brick. This all stuck out from beneath them and made the pile of wood level so the rusted metal chairs, rotted couches and settees stayed in place.

More pallets made a haphazard pyramid near the front door. Only the brave would tackle the stairs. You had to be careful not to put your foot through a space where the rotted slats left holes or to let one of the chair legs slide off into an abyss.

The rest of the place mirrored the style of the porch. Dogs wandered around, lay asleep or licked and scratched themselves. The mutts looked unhealthy. He kept them a little hungry and beat them now and then. He wanted them mean and cautious of humans in case someone came through the woods. No one could find the children. It would be the end of his project.

News moved around the Ozarks at lightning speed. Within a day, everyone in the area knew about the girl abandoned on Bear Road. Someone told Cletus this morning when he went to town for cigarettes.

For seventeen years, he stole children and released them by himself. He never used the word, kidnapped. This time he sent Boyd, the half-witted boy, to release the girl. What a mistake. Boyd dropped the kid within ten miles of the cabin.

Cletus thought he had life figured out. There were the victims and the predators. Growing up he had no choice but to be the victim. In his adult life, he chose a better option for himself.

Rage consumed him when he heard about the girl. "Boyd!" He kicked the rickety door of the cabin so hard, it came off the hinges and landed in front of him as he stepped out onto the porch. "Boyd! Where are you boy?"

"I'm right here." The young man stood near the edge of the yard.

"I let you take one of the children back to their parents. Tell me how it went."

"Okay. I put her out in Lindell, right next to a bar so someone would find her."

"What did you do with the crate and chain?" The more he lied, the tighter the man clinched his teeth together. "What if I told you someone found the girl about ten miles from here, still chained to the crate."

"I'm sorry. I got confused. I set out to take her to Lindell. On the way, I went into Potterville to Dinah's for a burger. When I came out, two men were trying to look in the back of the truck. I got scared and put her out on the darkest road I could find. I didn't think anyone would be out there, with the rain and fog and all." The boy looked down at his feet.

Courtney Hamilton, the girl in question had been on the mountain for four weeks. He took her from a clothing store in Davenport, Iowa. Her mother let her go window-shopping by herself. To go from one window to the next, she had to go around a slight curve in the wall. It put her out of the sight of her mother.

He grabbed her. It surprised him how unaware people were of what went on right under their noses. Moreover, the children were pliable. It only took a couple of words to keep them quiet. "If you make a sound, I'll kill your mother." or, "Be quiet, if you want to see your mother again."

He parked in handicap parking and always had a new car. This one he took only moments before from a grocery store parking lot six blocks away. People never remembered what new cars looked like; they were similar in body and style. Old cars had distinctive markings, bumper stickers or parking permits on the windows. It made them easier to remember.

After seventeen years of honing his craft, he knew he could take anyone from anywhere and get away with it. One of his fantasies had him working for the CIA, where they would pay him to catch spies. Now he let a boy have some responsibility and it ruined everything.

"Do you realize what this means? It means we have to leave our home. It hasn't been twenty-four hours and everyone knows about the girl. It will only be a day or two before they figure out where we are. What do you think your punishment should be?"

While Cletus talked to Boyd, Warren, his younger brother, walked out of the woods about twenty yards behind the teenager.

The first boy he took so long ago had stayed seventeen years. Both brothers wanted to let him go but Boyd begged to stay. Because of him, the seasoned kidnapper now watched each child for hours before he took one. He wanted to avoid taking another challenged child.

The boy was tolerable, and it helped to have a servant through the years. The kid acted strange, never looked anyone in the eye and swayed when he stood still. Cletus never cared one way or the other about him or anyone else. He prided himself on the fact he could gut shoot anyone, walk away, and never give them a second thought. Of all of his admirable traits, he felt it served him the best in life.

Because of the boy, they would have to flee. Everyone ought to be able to sense his superior intellect and follow his directions verbatim. When they strayed from his exact orders, it meant they lacked loyalty and Cletus could not stomach a traitor.

The consequences Boyd suffered through the years when he diverted from his exact task should have been enough to persuade him to follow the man's directions meticulously.

Cletus Compton had a total disregard for authority, and everyone else except for his mama in Georgia. A twinge of affection for his younger brother slipped through occasionally, but not often. They were the only two people in his life.

The boy stood there, head bowed toward his chest, scuffing his foot on the bare ground. Warren walked closer to his back, the entire time his older brother talked.

On signal; he reached out, grabbed Boyd by the neck and snapped it like a twig. The boy fell to the ground, dead.

Several of the children gave an audible gasp. Cletus took two huge steps in their direction and grinned when he saw the small heads duck into the boxes and stay there. "Stupid kids," he turned and walked back to the door.

They left the body where it fell. Warren went to feed the kids, and his brother went inside to get the items he deemed important and put them in the truck.

By the time he had the truck loaded, Warren stood beside him. "Well big brother, what's your plan?"

"We should burn the place to the ground to destroy any evidence."

"What if it causes a forest fire and burns the kids? We should unchain them so they have a chance."

"No. If they die up here, all the better for us." He grinned his yellow toothed grin.

Warren threw his belongings into the bed of the truck.

Together they dragged Boyd's body inside the cabin, pulled chairs, pallets, and firewood in on top of him and poured gasoline on all of it. They made a trail of gasoline and set it on fire as they left.

Time to pay Mama a visit.

It would be best to put as many miles as they could between them and Cherokee Ridge. The fire would spread rapidly. Someone would see the flames or smoke and come to investigate. Once the authorities found the kids, and they would, the whole area would be a circus.

They heard the whoosh of the accelerant as it met the dry fuel of the cabin. "Yippee." Cletus yelled as the truck bounced down the rocky path toward the main county road.

In Mt. Vernon, they stopped at Walmart for some clothes. They both had a five-day stubble and shaved in a Quick Stop bathroom, dyed their hair with cheap comb through dye for men and admired themselves in the plastic mirror.

The two of them were a distinctive pair, one with bright red hair and the other as white as a ghost. When Cletus wanted to make his brother angry, he called him, "Whitey."

The changes they made to their appearances made them stand out more than ever. People stared at them. When they noticed, others looking at them they would stare at the person until he or she looked away.

In Joplin, the pair rented a hotel room, took a nap, showered then put on their new clothes.

"Have you noticed how people look at us?" Warren asked.

"Yeah, what about it?" Cletus began to roll his old clothes in a ball and stuff them in a trash bag he pulled out of the waste can in the bathroom.

"We need to cut our hair. The dye didn't cover your ponytail and my hair is so dark, I look unreal." Warren added his clothes to the bag. When they left the room, they put it in a dumpster behind the restaurant next door.

He took the blade out of the razor and cut Warrens hair. "Not bad," he said when he saw it. His now, short black hair, no longer over shadowed his features.

When Warren cut his brother's hair he left it longer in the back. Cletus grumbled as he walked over to the bed and took five thousand dollars from a duffel bag.

A white Dodge pickup parked on a used car lot off Range Line Road caught their attention. All the television and radio stations and cops had a description of the old truck by now, the only choice was to ditch it. In an effort to slow the authorities down, they took the old truck out in the country, poured gasoline on it and watched it burn.

To backtrack through Lindell and head to Atlanta by a southern route seemed like the right move.

CHAPTER THREE

Tony made it home around nine a.m. He spent the rest of the night before with Courtney Hamilton and Thelma at the hospital in Lindell where the girl had a complete physical, and several shots.

Other than malnutrition, lice, and tick bites, she faired pretty well. Before they left the hospital, the doctor wanted Courtney to have a round of IV antibiotics, and some fluids to boost her strength.

Tony stripped to his jockey shorts and climbed into bed for a nap before he signed in at the office. Fifteen minutes later the radio on his night table came to life. Someone reported a fire on Cherokee Ridge. His deputy said they received fifteen calls in ten minutes. A massive out of control fire burned on the mountaintop. The wind blew from the North, which meant the fire would travel toward town.

No time for a nap now. The radio crackled

again and he listened to the mutual aid calls going out to the six closest towns. High Prairie had a volunteer fire department but the men had day jobs. It would to be up to the neighboring departments to douse the flames.

Tony could smell smoke and see the fire from his driveway. Sirens cut the quiet September morning as the fire crews headed toward the mountain. It earned the name because a Native American sacred burial ground lay on and beneath it. No one could build on sacred land.

By the time he arrived, over a hundred acres lay in ash. The heat kept firefighters from getting close enough to investigate the cause of the fire. Tony radioed the Highway Patrol office and asked for a helicopter to fly over and survey the situation.

About an hour later, his radio popped on. "Sheriff, can you hear me?"

"Sure, go ahead." Tony put his finger in his other ear to drown out some of the noise.

"Some kind of building has burned to the ground. If anyone got caught inside, they didn't survive. There are several dogs, tethered to crates. Looks like the biggest ones are trying to pull their cages away from the fire. If they keep going they will all fall off the cliff on the North side. The wind is shifting, too hot for us to stay here any longer. See you on the ground. Over and out."

"Roger that." Tony answered, but the radio went silent. Blood drained from his face and he felt sick. Those were not dogs up there and he knew it. In a steady voice he called on his men to go to the far side of the hill and try to save the children. The sheriff ran to his car and drove as far up the hill as he could. He weaved in and out of trees clipping the side of the door more than once. He ignored the damage and kept driving.

His mind raced. More children? Who would do such a thing? They did this right under his nose and within ten miles of his own house. What else went on in these Ozark Mountains?

As his Chevy Tahoe pulled the steep hill, the trees thinned out. When he looked up he saw them, six or seven crates with terrified children attached. Between him and the children, a shear granite cliff stuck out. Beneath it a drop off about fifty yards made it impossible for him to go any closer.

He needed the help of men with gear and he needed it before the children reached the edge of the cliff. Their terrified screams died in the wind. However, with the crackle of the timber as it burned and the whirl of the chopper blades, he could sense the cries.

The boxes moved ever so slowly toward the bluff.

He stood there helpless when one of the kids came into sight near the edge of the overhang. She had enough momentum to slide on over. In less than five seconds, she lay dead about a hundred feet away with parts of the crate on top of her.

Two firefighters came up to Tony's left and stood rooted for a second. "Are those children hooked to those boxes?" Tony thought it an observation more than a question.

"Hey, kids! Stop!" A firefighter shouted. His words too, were lost in the noise.

Tony ran back to his vehicle and honked the horn repeatedly. Each time he honked longer. It took a while, but the children began to look down toward the three men. All three shook their heads and waved their arms indicating the kids should stand still.

The firefighters ran around the end of the drop off, threw grappling hooks up as far as they could and began to climb. Their progress was slow and deliberate, but now instead of pulling toward the edge, the kids stood still and watched the men climb.

Water dropped from planes overhead to try to douse the fire. It slowed the rescue down and added to the slime from the moss and ice already present.

Other than hindering the firefighters' assent, the water did little. When it hit the fire, it sizzled only to have the fire flare up and roar a moment later. The first firefighter reached the top. Tony watched the man talk to each child in turn.

Within moments, the second firefighter joined his partner at the top. They separated each kid from their crate. Once the children were free, they herded them into a tight circle and had them sit. The first responders tied a rope around one girl, and lowered her down the rock wall where Tony grabbed her legs and guided her to the ground. The firefighters pulled the rope up and repeated the processes five more times until the kids were all at the bottom. After the last child made it safely, they repelled down to join them.

The sun had dropped below the mountaintop before Tony got word the fire was contained.

Smoke hung in the low places. The smell of burnt brush and grass overpowered everything.

Tony had long forgotten about fighting the fire. All of his attention went to the children; he stayed with them until the paramedics made it up the hill to check them out.

Every chance he had, he spoke calm and quiet words of encouragement.

The girl who fell had an obvious broken neck. Her legs and arms hung off the cliff in unnatural positions. The other children, three boys and three girls, told him they called the girl, Meagan. No one knew her last name.

A couple of first responders put the dead girl on a stretcher, covered her with a sheet and took her down the hill. The other six kids walked behind. He thought the oldest child they rescued might be twelve. Tony felt helpless and angry.

The firefighters, who rescued the kids, sat at the bottom of the hill resting under a tree, away from the hustle and bustle. The sheriff walked up to thank them. "You guys were amazing. I want to thank you on behalf of those children for your skill and quick thinking."

"It's what we do." In unison they raised their water bottles in a mock salute.

"What do you suppose went on up there?" The firefighter, whose nametag read Captain Michael Rogers, asked.

"We aren't sure yet."

"I have two kids," the other one said. "I'll be holding them tight tonight."

Tony shook his head and moved on.

The people who began to fight the fire early in the morning were still there. A couple of the restaurants in town brought sandwiches and cokes. The Red Cross sent someone with water, crackers, and a kind word.

The cabin remained too hot to investigate. Seven armed guards patrolled the perimeter of the ridge until daylight when a forensic team would be back to comb over the entire place.

Of course, Tony would be with them.

CHAPTER FOUR

Both of the Compton brothers confused meanness with pleasure. "Want to have a little fun?" Cletus stood close to his brother so he could whisper in his ear. "You go inside and get us some snacks. I'm going to push that old Toyota down the hill and see if I can hit that new truck at the bottom. Want to bet on it?"

Warren sized up the situation. "I'll bet you a ten spot you can't." He went inside to pay for the gas. While he stood in line he watched as his brother took the old car out of gear and pushed it. It picked up speed as it went down the slight grade of the parking lot. When it smashed into the truck, the sound of glass and the crunch of metal echoed in the valley below.

When Warren heard it, he grabbed the items he wanted, without bothering to pay, and ran to the truck laughing. They hooped and hollered until they were out of sight of the station.

Once before, about five years earlier, they set out to see their mama. However, Cletus beat a man half to death in a bar near Marked Tree, Arkansas, because he called him "Red". They headed back to the mountain as fast as they could.

An announcer interrupted the music on the radio to tell the public about the fire, the children, and them.

"I told you it would have been better for me to kill those kids instead of letting them go. Now there are half dozen or more of them who can testify against us. Maybe we should go back."

Warren never wanted to go back. He hoped the further he got from Cherokee Ridge, the more he could relax. "I'm glad you let them go. I would have liked it more if you let them go after you collected the ransom. Children are innocent. If you want to punish someone, make it an adult."

Over the years, they lost one child to measles, another to a snakebite and some died because they were not strong enough to eat a mixture of animal grade oats and barley mixed with sorghum and corn. Cletus wanted to feed it to them raw, but he and the boy boiled it in a metal water trough until it turned soft enough to eat. Others couldn't survive the harsh Ozark winter without warm clothes. A thin blanket covered them some nights, other nights-nothing.

Warren built a fire in a burn barrel in the center of the circle of crates. The kids were too far away to get much benefit, and no one tended it at night when the temperatures were the lowest.

When a child died, Warren wanted to either take them back to civilization where the body would be found or bury them. Cletus wanted to burn them in the barrel so no one would ever find them.

After a long discussion, the brothers agreed Warren could bury the bodies so long as he did not mark the graves. It turned out to be the most difficult chore of his life. With nothing more than a pickaxe to loosen the soil and a rusted coffee can to scoop it out, he put each child to rest. Legend said that all bodies should face east toward the rising sun. It could have been nothing more than folklore, yet the concept made him feel good about himself.

Every child who spent time on the ridge, whether they lived or died, chipped another hole in Warren's heart. The first one died of exposure, an unnecessary death, as they all were.

Cletus took the boy's blanket because he cried too loud and increased the chances of detection. "Noise bothers me. Shut up now or I'll give you something to cry about."

When the other captives heard the angry words spilling from his mouth, they ducked into the crates and stayed there.

The place resembled a survivalist camp with all of the purple posting tape strung from tree to tree, no trespassing signs nailed at eye level and half-starved dogs roaming around .

When Boyd made rounds with food the next morning, the child lay dead at the bottom of the cold, rotten crate. Cletus growled, "I guess he won't put us in jeopardy again."

Warren knew the name, face and age of all the dead kids. They came to visit him in his dreams and turned them into nightmares. Sometimes they haunted him in the light of day.

He shocked himself by speaking aloud. "I hope this ordeal with kids is over. I hate it."

"You're a sissy." Maybe his older brother did know him. Hatred and violence never helped anyone or any situation. When he arrived on the mountain, he hunted daily. These days, a dead deer brought tears to his eyes.

Warren thought often about killing himself to put an end to the torment. A lesson he learned at church, as a child, reminded him to view Hell with respect. Heaven and Hell were not stories, but literal places. If you went to the hell Warren believed in, you had to do unspeakable acts in deplorable conditions for eternity. It kept him alive.

When his brother and mother were together, there were no boundaries. They felt rules and laws were for everyone but them. It took his already skewed view of the world from bad to worse and terrified him.

With cowardice came consequences. Those two belonged in prison for life. There are different kinds of cowards, those who turned into bullies and killers and those who are followers. The people he called family came with an abundance of meanness dished out in beatings, bed without supper, and confinement in a closet.

They crossed the Spring River at the Arkansas border, and stopped at Mammoth State Park. Cletus left the keys in the truck while they went inside the welcome center to take a leak, get something to drink and pick up a snack or two.

Warren started to say something about the keys, but thought better of it; shrugged his shoulders and followed his older brother into the souvenir shop.

A half hour later, when they were ready to leave, the truck was not there. "Somebody stole my truck! He had better be long gone because if I find him I'll kill him."

"You left the keys in it." As soon as the words left his mouth, Warren knew he made a mistake. Cletus grabbed him by the top of the shirt, twisted it at the neck so he couldn't get a breath and put his face right up to Warren's.

"I can kill you too, Whitey. Now help me find a car so we can get out of here." The lack of air got the best of Warren and when the pressure eased, he fell to his knees.

Cletus always told him stupid people did stupid things. All the problems people had in the world stemmed from stupid mistakes. To point out the truck had the keys in it and how it constituted a stupid mistake could have been a fatal.

Best to let it go, although the logic mirrored the justification he used as to why he kidnapped the children. "Dumb people make dumb mistakes. If a parent leaves their kid somewhere I can take them it's their fault not mine." Several cars pulled in and out of the parking lot. Folks came and went, but when he began beating the hood of a green Ford sedan near the exit, people rolled up their windows and looked the other way.

Cletus grabbed a woman out of her car and threw her to the pavement. "Get in the car, lamebrain. Let's get out of here."

In the next town, they spotted the truck with the keys still in it. Warren begged his brother. "Let's take our truck and go. It won't be long before the police show up."

"I'll handle the police. I bet the thief is in that café over there." As they passed the truck, Cletus reached in, grabbed his gun from the glove compartment and stuck it in his pants at the small of his back. "You coming, Whitey?"

"Don't call me that." Disdain burned in his belly.

The building sat at the south end of the parking lot. The windows had advertisements painted on them. Cletus pushed the door open. Warren reluctantly followed. The seats showed wear but the place sparkled and shined. Three men sat in a booth toward the back, actually, they were teenagers.

Cletus marched up, put both of his hands on the table and leaned in. "Which one of you geniuses stole my truck?"

"What truck?" A skinny kid asked then threw his head back and let out a belly laugh. "Should know better than to leave your keys in the ignition, old man."

Warren watched as his brother's face turned bright red then a dark crimson. It meant someone would die. He stepped to the side out of Cletus' line of vision and tried to signal for the kid to shut up.

The rest happened in an instant.

He took the gun out of his pants and waved it

around for a second. The boys scrambled to hide under the table, knocking chairs over but finding little cover. The first three shots caught the mouthy kid in the chest. As the boy bled out on the floor and the other two begged for their lives, Cletus took a half-eaten cheeseburger off one of the plates still on the table. With the burger in one hand and the gun in the other, he backed out the door. Once outside, he shot the rest of bullets into the plate glass windows as he ran to the truck.

Warren ran after him. They jumped in and headed toward Memphis.

He finished the burger and turned toward his brother. "You should have taken one of these. They're damn good."

The combination of grilled beef and onions mixed with the unmistakable smell of fresh, warm blood caused Warren to get the dry heaves.

He leaned his head out the side window to take a deep breath of fresh air, and then turned toward his brother. "We need to find another vehicle, and soon. Everybody in the state will be looking for us and a white Dodge with KC lights."

"You're right. What would you like to have? An SUV, a Cadillac, maybe a Hummer?"

"I'll take anything we don't have to hurt someone to get. Preferably something no one will report missing for a few days."

"What's wrong little brother, are you getting soft?" He laughed. "Oh, I mean softer."

Warren remained quiet. He stuck his head back out the window and breathed in the cool air.

They stole a Lincoln Continental from a detail

shop in Jonesboro and a license plate from a Chevy Malibu in a junkyard. The truck they left in an industrial park near the Riceland plant, hidden between two abandoned warehouses.

The entire ordeal exhausted him. He crawled into the backseat and lay down. Hopefully they would stop at a Memphis motel.

CHAPTER FIVE

Tony Massey felt tired, disappointed and disgusted with people. He rolled the windows down on his police cruiser on the drive back to town in hopes the fresh cool air would keep him awake. Twenty minutes later, he pulled into the parking lot at the office.

Cara Stafford shook her head at him when he walked in the door. "My goodness, Sheriff, sit down before you fall down. I'll get you some coffee."

Tony stumbled to his office and sat in the closest chair. "What did I miss?" He asked when Cara, his assistant, came back with their coffee.

"Nothing unusual. You had a court date yesterday to testify for Danny Thornton. I sent Randy." She handed him a steaming cup of muddy liquid they called coffee then walked on around to sit in his desk chair.

"Man, it didn't enter my mind." He rubbed the dark stubble on his chin.

"It went well. Danny got probation instead of jail time and he learned a valuable lesson."

"Good." Danny had a bright future if he could control his temper.

"Anything else?"

"Just about the cabin and the kids from the fire. Every news and media outlet within a thousand miles is either here or on their way. This morning our little county made the national news. We were on CNN, Good Morning America and the Today Show. As soon as the story about the kids, hit the airwaves, the phones started ringing. Every parent with a missing child has called or is trying to call, on the slim chance one of those kids is theirs." She shook her head. "I suggest we make a plan. Then you go home and take a nap before it gets even crazier around here. The FBI is on their way and if they get here before you leave, you will never get out of here." Cara talked fast as if she would forget something if she slowed down.

"Jeez. I wish I had a plan." He sat his cup on the edge of the desk and lowered his head to let his face rest in the palms of his hands.

"I canceled all time off and called in all personnel. Some of the men are on the phones in the break room. Others went outside to block off the square so we can establish a free zone where no one but those on official business can drive. I made up a form for our people on the phones to use so we have all the same information on each person who calls in about one of those children."

Tony looked up and smiled at her. "Cara, you always make me look good. It's difficult to know how much the FBI will let us be involved. I don't know if they will just look into the little prisoners or the entire mess."

"There are two men coming down from St. Louis and three from Tulsa. No one knows what to expect. You should go home and sleep. Get something to eat. I can cover this place for a few hours," She grinned. "It's my specialty."

Tony stood, stretched to his full height and stayed that way a minute. "I do need a nap. I won't be gone long. Page me if you need me."

Five minutes later, Tony pulled up to the speaker at the drive through of the local fast food place, ordered a burger and a Coke, and ate it on the way home.

He stripped down to his shorts and fell asleep shortly after his head hit the pillow.

At four o'clock, he got up, showered, dressed and went back to the office. Cara briefed him again. The FBI had arrived and went immediately to Cherokee Ridge to acclimate themselves to the scene. The phone bank they set up had logged over four hundred calls from people searching for lost children. The FBI had also sent support staff who helped with phone calls and did some of the grunt work.

Tony's anxiety lessened. "By the way, someone did see the person who dropped the girl and the crate on Bear Road. Two men were standing outside the convenience store in Porterville and saw a blue Dodge pickup pull into the lot. They noticed a large wooden crate in the back. It sat forward in bed of the truck." Cara smiled. "We're making progress."

Porterville, the smallest town in Ash County, had little to draw people to it. The only viable business, called Dinah's Pit Stop made pizza, had a small diner with a grill, rented movies and sold lottery tickets.

Cara continued, "A different truck, no one had seen before, would stand out like a movie star at the county fair. It piqued the local's curiosity. The men were heading to the back of the lot to check out the truck when the young man came out of the store. The two men tried to engage him in conversation. He wouldn't respond."

"Not much to go on." Tony stood.

"It gets better." Cara followed him into his office. "Before the young man left, one of them jotted down the plate number on the front of the truck. They called a little while ago and gave it to me- after they saw the morning news. I ran the number. It came back registered to a Warren Moss Compton, age 35, with box number in Condole, Georgia."

"I'd say something is wrong with the registration. There haven't been any box numbers allowed on ID's for years, not since the 911 system became active in 1968, ten years before this man was born." Tony loved to figure out clues. "We might need our FBI friends to do a check for us. They have a larger database."

"I'm way ahead of you, Sheriff. One of the FBI staff ran the name and address through Codas. It showed a clean record for Warren Compton. His license has been expired for ten years. After they searched the name further, they came up with associates at the same address. Cletus Beaufort Compton, age forty-two, probably a brother, who has a juvenile record but nothing as an adult. He has no arrest record after March of 1991. No change of address showed up, nor did records for a bank account, IRS forms, or medical records. There is a closed military record; they are working on getting it unsealed."

"Do we have an occupation?"

"No. It said 'unknown'. Most of the information is about their mother, Minnie Davis Compton, age 66. Her address is 2222 Rice Drive, Atlanta."

"Interesting. Do we have any pictures?" Tony asked.

"Yes, we do." Cara pulled out a picture of an albino male. "This is one of our subjects."

"Do we have any information on the woman?" Tony stood and took the picture of Minnie from Cara.

"Yes, her rap sheet would stretch around the block. Several arrests for child abandonment, child endangerment, prostitution, fraud, check kiting, drug possession with intent to sell and murder."

"It might answer to why the boys chose a life of crime."

"It might. She served fifteen years of her adult life incarcerated and seven on probation. They tried to put the boys in foster care but when they went to pick them up, they were gone. At the time they were ten and sixteen.".".

"Do the agents in the field know all of this?" Tony asked.

"Yes, one of the other agents drove out to talk to them."

"Ok, thanks, I am going out to the Ridge. Have the two men from Potterville drop by for a chat. Call Max in Lindell and ask him if we can borrow their sketch artist. Coordinate it with the witnesses." Tony turned and walked out the door.

The FBI personnel wore navy blue jackets with FBI printed in white block letters about six inches high on the back and left chest and a baseball hat to match.

"Agent Juan Gomez," a man said as he extended his hand. "I'm here from Tulsa to help you clean up and solve this crime. Agent Ben Goodman is from the St. Louis office."

Once the pleasantries were over, they got right to it. "Sheriff, you've got a mess up here."

"I know. Where do we start?" Tony asked.

"I'd say getting those kids reunited with their families." Gomez turned toward Goodman. "I hate these cases. The smell of charred flesh, men mean enough to hurt children, and devastated parents. The kind that keeps me up at night."

Tony took a deep breath and smelled it for the first time. He would never forget it.

The only sounds were CSI and the rest of the FBI team scraping through the rubble and ash.

Tony walked further away from the scene to lean on his SUV. "I have some news. The night before the fire, a woman found a child chained to a crate like those." The sheriff pitched his head toward the boxes. "You know about the men who saw a young man driving a truck with a box in the back. They got the tag number off the vehicle. We ran the plate and we have a name."

The two FBI agents looked at one another. "Can the men tell us about the driver?"

"We heard some of it. You know how it is. Details get lost in translation," Gomez said.

"If you want to interview them, they will be at the office by the time we get there."

"I don't want to miss that," Ben said.

Tension and excitement energized High Prairie. Tony's men had cordoned off the town square and one block around it. The one way in, one way out traffic pattern worked well and kept spectators far enough away the county and city could function without interruption.

Satellite television trucks lined the streets, outside the barriers. Personalities, some of whom Tony recognized, jockeyed to get as close as they could to the agents and the sheriff as they exited their vehicles.

"Go throw them a bone, Sheriff. We need to keep them on our side."

Tony hated undue attention, but he went over to give the media a statement "This will go better," he said to the entire group. "If you do not ask questions at this point." No one stepped back. One friendly face in the crowd he recognized from the local station in Lindell. He moved over and talked directly to her.

After the noise settled down he spoke in a clear

steady voice no one had to strain to hear. "This is the situation as of now. We found six children on Cherokee Ridge. Another girl, abandoned on Bear Road is in good spirits and resting in an undisclosed location. One child, a girl, died at the scene of the fire. In total, eight children are involved now and evidence gives us reason to believe several dozen more were involved over a long period. The seven children are in protective custody." Tony looked at the faces in front of him to see if they understood the horror of what he said. Most did. "A cabin on the Ridge was a total loss. Authorities found a body in the rubble. We will give more details as they become available." As soon as he finished his statement, he turned and walked away. Goodman and Gomez waited for him near the door.

Tony looked around as they walked in. The hustle, bustle and noise could unsettle the calmest of people. Cara greeted them and briefed them on the events at the office while they were on the Ridge.

"The men from Porterville are in your office. I set you men up in the conference room." She acknowledged the FBI agents. "Your people brought in computers. The FBI office support people are in the break room with some of our people still taking phone calls. There are hundreds. Tony, I left your seldom used items in your office and put the extra laptop in the conference room in case you want to work with them." She nodded toward the agents a second time.

"Nice job, Cara."

Juan chose to go in with the other agents and

check their progress, specifically, information on Warren Compton. Ben went with Tony to interview the men from Porterville.

"This is Agent Ben Goodman with the FBI," Tony said when they met the men.

Cara opened the door and offered to get everyone coffee. Noise invaded the room and made it impossible for them to hear anything. "Just close the door, we won't be long," Tony said, "I understand you men saw a young man in a blue Dodge pickup with a crate in the back. I'd like for you to tell us more about the incident."

"Well, we meet daily at Dinah's, morning and evening. At dusk, the kid drove up. He had a crate in the back of a blue Dodge pickup. He had it backed up to a telephone pole."

"Yeah," The other man chimed in. "You can't miss the kid. He sways when he stands and never looks straight at anyone. There's something wrong with him."

"His name's Boyd," the second man said.

"I'm a little confused here. I thought you didn't know the boy in the truck. That he drove up and you were curious so you looked in the back." Ben stood as he talked. "Now you know his name. What did I miss?"

"Well, since we saw the boy that night, and Cherokee Ridge burned, it's all anyone talks about. Then we heard about the other kids and the other crates. People said they knew there was something strange about those three."

"What three?" Tony shrugged toward Ben.

The second man, Terry, chimed in. "The two

men and the boy, Boyd."

"So you know who Boyd and the other men are?" Tony asked.

"No, like I said, we heard about them. George over at the MFA said two men came in once a week. The boy came with them…"

"Jeez," Tony said. He and Ben left. "Cara, put these guys with the artist, and then let them go."

The feed store had to be the busiest place around. Most people in the area were farmers. The store buzzed with excitement when the Sheriff and Ben, still in his FBI jacket, walked in.

"George, I need to talk to you, in the office." They walked toward a room in the back of the store.

"Sounds serious, Sheriff, what can I do for you?"

"Tell me about the two men and the boy who came in here every week."

"Well, the one guy, about forty I'd say, was unpleasant. He didn't talk much and when he did it was snarly."

"Describe him to me," Ben said.

"About six feet tall, skinny with bright red hair. Actually, it was orange when the sun hit it. It would have been pretty on a girl."

Ben and Tony glanced at one another. "Did he have any scars or anything unusual about him?"

"He always paid in cash. Now, the other fella was unusual. One of those albinos." George rubbed his head.

"Is this the man?" Tony showed him the picture of Warren Compton they got from the DMV.

"Yep, that is the younger of the two. Warren

was his name."

"Tell me about the boy," Ben said.

"I'd say he was seventeen or eighteen, he swayed when he stood. He never looked at anyone, just kept his eyes to the ground. The older guy, Cletus, yelled at him like he was a dog."

"So the other man's name was Cletus?" Tony had a tone this time.

"I thought I told you their names, Cletus, Warren, and Boyd. Even though their coloring was so different, you could spot the two older ones as brothers. I don't know how the kid fit in."

Tony felt like he had to work too hard for some simple information. He looked up and all the people had drifted back near the office and stood watching him, Ben, and George.

Had there been a door he would have closed it.

"Okay George, tell me what they bought when they came here. Tell me anything else you can remember of about them," Ben said.

"Well, they always came in the morning before we got busy. They drove a blue extended cab Dodge pickup with a rebel flag decal on the back bumper. They bought the same thing every week, fifty pounds of oats, fifty pounds of corn feed, two pounds of sorghum, a bag of barley and a Hersey bar for Boyd."

Now they had names. They knew Warren had white hair from his picture. They needed a photo of the older one.

"I bet Boyd is the body in the cabin," Ben said as they got back to the office.

Noise assaulted them when they opened the

door. Tony hated noise. He lived alone, and loved quiet. He never played music at home and rode around all day, alone in his car. Too much commotion unsettled him

Tony looked in all the rooms to see what the men worked on. There had to be a better way to do this. He could never work in this chaos.

"Follow me," he said to Ben and Juan. A moment later, they were on an elevator that went downstairs to the jail or upstairs to an outdoor smoking area on the roof. They went up. Silence, fresh air, high fences and bars made up the area. Tony tried to relax. He walked over to the fence and looked down. Below him satellite trucks, portable generators, bright lights and now food trucks lined the streets. What a circus.

Ben and Juan walked up behind him. Ben put his hand on Tony's back.

Tony shook his head. "I never thought about something major happening in Ash County."

"No one ever does. They know it can't happen where they live. When it does, the small town innocence is lost." They stood quietly, each absorbed in their own thoughts.

Tony left to interview the children who were rescued from the Ridge."

Ben said he would organize the phone messages.

Juan headed for the morgue to see about the dead girl and the body from the cabin. "Why don't you stop by the morgue with me on the way to the hospital?" Juan asked Tony.

CHAPTER SIX

Cletus loved and trusted his mama. The closer he got to home, the better he felt. It wouldn't be long now. Once at home, with Mama's help, he would come up with a plan to leave the country. He sucked on a toothpick and hummed to himself.

Wherever he went, he would go alone. He could only take so much of his candy-ass sissy brother. When the first child died on the Ridge, Warren changed. 'I am my brother's keeper', had to be for people who had cowardly brothers like his.

Warren nagged him to let the kids go. To keep a child for one day increased the chances of detection, to chain them to a wooden crate, half-starve them and let them go later bordered on insanity, Warren would say repeatedly.

How many times did he need to repeat it? It made perfect sense. You take kids, get the money and then punish the parents for their carelessness. The children should never been left somewhere they would be in harm's way. He told Warren, "If they left a kid in a hot car, they would be punished to the full extent of the law. I punish them for being stupid and not keeping an eye on them in public."

Cletus' mom put him in the closet when she went out. She said to protect him she would have to lock him up. She told him it would destroy her if anyone took him while she ran one of her "errands". At first, it made him angry, but after a while, he realized his mother loved him enough to lock him up to keep him safe.

It all changed one day when he and his mom came home from a particularly good day, and found a six-year-old on the porch. When he saw how upset it made Mama, he walked over and kicked the crap out of the boy. After a bit, Mama said, "Don't kill him, he's your brother."

The kid turned out to be okay. Cletus needed a follower and Warren fit the bill. They became close, but not so close he couldn't kill his newly found brother if he felt the need.

He still went with his mama as much as he could and his new brother went to the closet. "Fairs fair," he would say when he locked him in.

On several occasions, Mama left both boys for weeks. She would come back tanned, much thinner, tired and meaner than before she left. However, the time she spent at home, she spent with Cletus. She put him next to her in her bed and snuggled with him. It meant she loved him the best. He had the world's best mom.

Warren became an inconvenience for him, but he could manipulate the boy with fear, and it kept him entertained.

Mama went to prison before the boys could legally live on their own. Some people came to the house to see about them. The boys hid under the porch. They heard every word those people said about their mama being a whore, a crack head and a menace to society. She shot and killed a man while jacked up on coke. Cletus figured the man deserved it. It didn't surprise Warren in the least that his mom killed someone.

The bottom line, Mama would not be home any time soon.

Cletus took his brother, the car, all the money in the house and left Atlanta.

They roamed around the country for nearly two years. They robbed old women as they came home from church, grabbed money out of cash registers and stole cars and gasoline.

One day Cletus saw a news story about a kidnapped girl whose parents paid a ransom of fifty-thousand dollars to get her back.

He knew exactly what to do.

They became squatters and moved into an old abandoned cabin on top of Cherokee Ridge, in the heart of the Ozarks.

Cletus grew tired of his brother, who spent his time learning to track, hunt with a knife and draw pictures of the animals and birds he saw. Warren tied a hunting knife on his lower leg with a bright yellow bandana and only took it off to bathe and change clothes.

He spent an exorbitant amount of time fine-tuning his money making plan. He couldn't find his brother when he got ready to leave the first time so he went by himself. At a mall in Toledo, Ohio, he walked around the shops and food court for several hours, until he spotted a woman sitting in front of a Chinese restaurant reading a book. A small boy played under the table at her feet. The child would mosey away two or three tables and then go back to his mother.

For over an hour, he watched the mother and the child. He had to make his move or leave. The longer he hung around, the greater the chance someone would notice him. The boy needed to wander a bit further from his mother for Cletus to execute his plan. After months of meticulous preparation, he wasn't going to get in a hurry and screw it up.

Once he had the child, he tossed him in the trunk of a car he stole from a commuter parking lot a mile away. Within minutes, he heard sirens wail as the police headed for the shopping center. He waited for them to pass. The rush he got as car after car of police skidded up to the mall doors with sirens blaring gave him a hard on.

People began to gather. In much less time than he expected, they put the mother on TV so she could beg for her son back. She told about how her child disappeared from right under her nose.

"No." She did not see anyone strange hanging around. No one saw anything. "My boy, Boyd, is special needs. He must take his daily medicine to keep him from having seizures. I implore you please bring my boy back. I won't call the police or press charges against you."

"Yeah, right," he said under his breath as he sat in the local Waffle House and sipped a hot cup of coffee. He let the boy go hungry.

Cletus missed the Ridge, but he waited and stuck to his plan to retrieve the ransom. For five nights he slept in his car out in the country before he stole a phone and made the call for the money.

Not once did Warren come to mind. He focused only on his task. In order to be a success, you must be smarter than the people trying to catch you. Not once in his life did he doubt his intellectual superiority.

All of his life he out foxed, out smarted and out maneuvered the people he met.

He got out, found a small stick, whittled it into a toothpick, stuck in his mouth then yelled, "Yippee!" as loud as he could.

The boy remained in the trunk of the car most of the time except when Cletus let him out to eat a candy bar and some chips and pee if he had to. On the sixth day, he drove back to Toledo and watched the news.

The tree trunks, telephone poles, shop windows and bulletin boards in town had pictures of Boyd Baxter and a plea to the kidnapper not to hurt him.

They still cried about the medicine the boy needed. The child survived fine without it. They said it, he decided, to force him to make a mistake.

He laughed and laughed.

"Twenty-four hours, ten thousand dollars and no police or your boy is dead," Was all Cletus said into the phone, along with the exact location to put the money.

The drop directions were simple and clear. They could follow them or not. It made no difference to him. He gutted rabbits, squirrels, and cats and dogs all of his life. A boy would not be any different to him.

"Put the money in a zippered bank bag. Leave it in the drainage ditch at the end of Madison Road then drive north and turn east at Campbell Drive."

"Where can we pick up our boy?" He detected a wobble of emotion in the father's voice.

"After I have the money, and no police are involved, I will let you know where you can pick him up. If you don't follow these directions exactly, I will kill Boyd and send him back to you in twenty little pieces. Do you understand?"

He arrived four hours early, climbed a giant maple tree with a canopy so thick no one could see him from the ground,, he waited and watched.

Right on time, a man drove up, dropped a bag in the ditch, looked around, returned to his car and drove slowly away. He watched as the man proceeded down the street. No one came after him. In the twilight, he scooted down the tree trunk, jogged to the ditch, picked up the money and left.

He went through a back yard and then another until he came upon the stolen car he took hours before. Six blocks later he abandoned the second car, and got into another one he had waiting. That one he drove to the mall where he picked up one more, car just to be safe.

An hour later, he drove into a commuter

parking lot, switched to the car with the boy in the trunk, and drove toward Missouri. Two hours later, he transferred the boy to the toolbox in the back of his truck and drove home humming his favorite Queen song.

No one came after him. No one caught him. Damn, he committed the perfect crime. Cletus was on a high like never before. He drove back to Cherokee Ridge as soon and as fast as he could get there.

Warren waited for him with new stories of his adventures in the mountains. Kidnapped kids were not his thing and he wanted no part of it.

Seventeen years and no one had a clue how he made his money. Over the years, he took one hundred and thirteen children and over two million dollars.

The crime books he read said the undoing of many a thief lay in his inability to monitor spending. To keep from drawing attention to himself he drove an old vehicle, wore old clothes and never flashed large sums of money.

In one of the stories, five men robbed an armored truck. They had the perfect plan, split the money and went their separate ways. One of the men bought an expensive house, a yacht, and a new Cadillac in the same year. He became the subject of an IRS investigation, and when he was arrested, he made a deal for no jail time and ratted on the other four men. They were serving twenty-five years to life at a high security prison.

He doled money out to Warren, twenty or thirty dollars at a time and paid for his cigarettes and groceries with small denomination bills.

Not once did Cletus Compton ever question what he did, including feeling bad about the people he killed, the kids who died or the money he stole. He lived a charmed life and he knew it.

No one could catch him.

No one could kill him.

CHAPTER SEVEN

Dr. Jamison stood over the lifeless body of the girl who fell from the ledge. "So far," he said. "I know she was dehydrated, and malnourished." He lifted the child's arm up off the table and showed the men the lack of elasticity in her skin. "From the marks on her wrist, I would say she had the chain around it for several months. You will have my full report by tomorrow"

After the morgue, the sheriff went to Moxie Hospital to spent time with the victims. They ranged in age from five to eleven. Tony began with the oldest. "Hi, son, I'm Tony Massey the county sheriff. Can you tell me your name and perhaps where you're from?"

"Austin Murray. I'm from Wichita, Kansas."

"How did you end up chained to a cage on a mountain top?" Tony sat on the edge of the boy's hospital bed.

"I was on my way home from baseball practice. A man came out of nowhere. He picked me up and threw me in the trunk of a car. I didn't have time to run." Austin began to cry.

"It's okay, you're with us now. It doesn't sound like there was anything you could do. You say there was only one man?"

"When I got put in the car there was only one, a red-headed man with a ponytail."

Tony showed him a picture of Warren Compton. "Is this him?"

"No. That's Warren. The man who took me is Cletus. Did you catch him?"

"Not yet, but the entire country is looking for him. He can't stay hidden long."

"Why did he take me?"

"People like him find children alone, then take them to get money from their parents."

"Did my parents give him money?"

"I'm sure they did."

"I sure would like to see my mom and dad, but he told me if I got away or go home any other way than him taking me, he will kill my family." Austin wiped his thin cheek with the back of his hand.

"We can keep you safe. Those men are long gone."

"I don't know what to do. I want to see my parents, but I don't want anything else to happen to any of us."

"FBI and I can keep you safe, I promise." Tony patted the youngsters shoulder.

"Cletus said you would say that. He said he

would be back when I least expected it." The boy's eyes filled with tears. "I'll just stay here until someone catches him. Tell Mom and Dad I am okay."

"Let's talk about it later. I would like to ask you a few more questions."

"Okay." The boy moved away from Tony and pulled the blankets up until he resembled a turtle afraid to come out of his shell.

Tony stood to give the boy some breathing room. "Did those men hurt you?"

"Yes and no. They put a chain on my wrist, made me sleep in a wooden box with no lid, and fed me some crap that looked and smelled like somebody already ate it." The boy never loosened his grip on the blanket.

"Did they ever hit you or touch you?" Tony nodded toward the boy's lower body.

"No, no. They didn't do anything like that. A younger man, the blonde; actually, his hair is white, but not the color of old people's hair. He took care of us."

"You said their names were Cletus and Warren. Can you describe Cletus to an artist so he could draw us a picture of him?"

"Sure I can. There was a third man, a teenager. This name was Boyd Baxter."

"How do you know his last name?"

"The man, Cletus, would scream at him. When he did, he threatened to kill him and always called him by his whole name, Boyd Allen Baxter. They finally killed him."

"Did you see them kill him?" Tony took a step

closer.

"The day of the fire, Warren came up behind Boyd and stood there a long time. Cletus yelled at the kid about ten minutes then Warren grabbed him by the neck and turned it real fast. Boyd fell to the ground and never moved again. Before they left, they dragged him inside the cabin and set it on fire." The boy began to shake and cried again.

"Is there anything else you want to tell me, Austin?"

He wiped the tears with the back of his hand. "Yes. You don't understand about Cletus. Every night, he went from box to box and lifted each of us up by one arm or our hair or neck. He told us he would find us no matter where we went or how much time passed. We were to stay where we were until he took us home."

"I know, but he left you on top of a mountain in a raging fire. Doesn't that change things? He left you to die and didn't try to take you home."

"Sheriff, I can't take the chance. Every day I made a scratch on the inside of the box so I could keep track of the time I stayed in the box."

"And how long was it?"

"Seventy-six days, the day of the fire's when I made my last mark."

"You're a brave boy. I'm not sure I could do it. Is there anything else you want to tell me before I go?" Tony shook his head. "I don't want anything to happen to you or your parents. I will repeat everything you said to the FBI agents on the case. However, men like those two are usually cowards. There's an officer outside your door, one at the elevator and several downstairs. If you remember anything else, you want to tell me, let one of the officers know. We will call your parents tonight and tell them you're safe."

"But I am NOT safe! Don't you understand that's what I've been telling you? He will come after me, or have Warren kill me like he did Boyd."

Tony felt sorry for what Austin was going through. The boy truly thought Cletus could get to him, even when he was surrounded by officers. "You're not goin to die on my watch. Okay?" Finally Austin nodded and Tony left the room.

The other children at the Moxie were able to give Tony additional information. A nine-year-old girl, Heather Newcastle, came from Denver.

Tony pulled the visitor's chair up to end of the bed and sat down. "How long were you on the mountain Heather?"

"Three weeks and maybe a week in the trunk of a car."

Cletus had picked her up outside her school while she waited for her dad, who was half an hour late. Her story mirrored the one Austin told. She said she couldn't go home without Cletus or he will kill her parents and her little brother. These kids were brainwashed. Heather also saw Warren kill Boyd the day of the fire.

Tony couldn't fathom people like the ones he heard about all day He found out Cletus left the mountain alone to get the children. When he left the mountain, Warren helped the kids by feeding them fruit and vegetables.

The sheriff took copious notes, but he knew no matter what happened in his life or how many cases he had, he would never forget these kids, what they said, how they looked or the fear they emitted.

The other three children there were younger. They were afraid of him. Daniel Degras and Joe Gray said they were from San Antonio and Reno. The little girl hid her head and wouldn't talk. The boys told him her name was Mary. She moved to the far side of the bed and faced the window. He thought she looked four or five. Tony sat in a chair on the other side of the room. He avoided words he thought might scare her. He told her no one could get to her to hurt her and assured her, her parents would be there soon.

Daniel told him there were usually about five or six kids on the hill at one time but in the last couple of months, Cletus left a lot and brought kids back every week or so. "Tell my parents I love them, but I can't go home. He swore he would come get me again and kill my family." Daniel insisted.

Tony reassured him, "The boy is dead and the men are gone. They were last seen hundreds of miles from here. It is perfectly safe for you to go home with your parents."

"You can't make me." Daniel turned toward the wall.

Joe Gray also related Boyd's murder to Tony. He added a few details about a typical day. When it got too cold, Warren wrapped the crates with plastic. If the plastic tore though, he didn't bring more. Once he came into camp with blankets and gave them each two. But if you did something

Cletus deemed bad, he would take away a blanket. If you lost both blankets, you could freeze. He too said he would not go home. Fear ran through each of the children and bonded them in the decision to sacrifice their happiness to protect their families.

Tony thought he had all the information he needed and headed for the elevator. A nurse stopped him and said the littlest girl wanted him to come back to her room.

"My name is Mary," she said in a husky voice. "Mary Campbell. I don't remember where I live." She began to cry. The sheriff walked over and sat down with her.

"Nice to meet you, Mary Campbell. I want you to know, that's all the information I need to find your parents."

"Really?" She smiled for a moment but it faded. She kept her eyes on him. "I miss them. I wish I could go home."

"You can," Tony said.

"No, I can't. They will come after me and kill my family."

"Would it make you feel better to know they are gone?" Tony asked

"Are they dead?"

"No, Mary, but they are far away from here. They won't bother you again."

"I don't want to take the chance…"

Once in his cruiser, Tony beat his hands on the steering wheel. "I'm going to get these bastards."

He headed for his place on the outskirts of town. Since this case began, he'd been restless. Each night he cleared the house commando style, gun loaded, arms extended, and flashlight in hand. In his line of work, he couldn't be too careful. Besides, the Compton brothers made the hair on the back of his neck stand up.

Once he checked the doors, secured the windows he headed for the shower. His plan included a couple of beers and a ballgame. The St. Louis Cardinals and Kansas City Royal were tied two games each in a series the press called the, I 70 series.

He put on a pair of pajama pants and a long sleeve tee shirt. That's all he remembered. He woke up three hours later, stiff and sore from sleeping in a chair.

CHAPTER EIGHT

Tony and the agents met at Lilly's Diner on the square for breakfast. As they sat talking, the two agents' phones rang at the same time. About ten seconds later, so did Tony's.

"Sheriff, Cara here. Seems the Compton brothers bought a different truck in Joplin, burned the old one in a Best Buy parking lot and headed right back through Lindell toward, who knows where."

"Do we have a positive ID?" Tony could hear a little of the other conversations and knew their calls were about the same subject.

"Yes, and that's not all. The manager of a restaurant found their clothes in a dumpster. The man at the car lot described them to a tee. They have cut their hair and attempted to dye it."

"How do you know they came back this way?"

"Because Cletus assaulted a women in the parking lot of a souvenir shop in the state park at the Missouri, Arkansas border and killed a man in Hardy, Arkansas. They were last seen heading east, toward Memphis. They're in a white 2011 Lincoln Continental. Someone got the plate number but it's not a match to the car. The Memphis police are checking out motels and hotels along the main highways.".."

"Thanks, Cara."

"I'll keep you posted."

"Roger that."

"I guess you got the same call we did?" Juan asked. "The Compton boys are out of control. I'd say they are headed to Georgia to see their mother. If they drive straight through they wouldn't arrive until tomorrow night."

"I'll fly down there and coordinate their capture." Ben stood and put his phone away.

"Don't go yet. I need to fill you in on my interviews with the kids." Tony motioned for Ben to sit back down. "Those kids are scared and in shock. They want to see their families but they say they can't go home. Cletus said he would kill them all if they went back without his help. They believed him."

"Jeez. I hate kidnapping cases. Thank goodness they are few and far between." Ben ran his hand through his thick brown hair.

"I notified all the parents about an hour ago," Juan said. "They should all arrive by tomorrow night. When they get here they will want to take their kids home with them

"Our job, first and foremost is to protect the victims and catch the criminals. I won't go to Atlanta. I'll let the local office take care of the capture and we will deal with the kids and the parents." Ben took out his note pad.

"We need a therapist, or a counselor. We could use a place to house the kids, their parents and we'll have to have guards."

Tony took his phone out and hit search. When what he wanted popped on his screen, he laid it on the table for the agents to see. "This is Camp Moccasin. It's closed for the season. I bet we can use it, put the kids there, along with their parents and the therapist."

"It might be the answer," Juan said. "We could move the entire operation there. It would get us out of the Sheriff's office and make it easier to keep an eye on everyone."

For the next two hours, Ben took care of the details in Atlanta; Tony got permission to use the Camp and arranged for a cook, food, linens and all the necessities. Juan called the Agency to see about a therapist.

Ben interrupted. "Remember that doctor, the one who walked into a hostage situation about ten years ago in St. Louis? The pretty lady who almost got cut in two by a crazy bank robber."

"How could I forget?" Juan said. "It was my first day on the job. When we stormed the bank I went over to help her. I couldn't believe it. So much blood and the perp dead, half laying on top of her."

"I heard she lives in the Ozarks. Maybe she would do it. It would be quicker and she is a trained agent," Ben said. "Do you remember her name?"

"I'll never forget her. Dr. Boo Jordan." Juan stood "Tony, do you know Dr. Jordan?"

"Sure I do. She's the one who found the first girl on Bear Road. She's retired FBI? She's famous around here because she writes self-help books."

"She was the best profiler in the FBI for years. Then, one day, she walked into a bank and tried to defuse a situation and free dozens of hostages. She said she knew immediately the man intended to kill everyone, including her and himself. Dr. Jordan pulled a derringer from her boot and shot him. He died, but not before he stabbed her in the belly. The knife sliced her liver and spleen. We all thought she would bleed out before the paramedics arrived. "

Tony had no idea. He first met Boo when a local man shot another man in the eye because he disrespected him in front of his friends. Boo happened to be in a bar in Lindell interviewing someone for her latest book and overhead the killer bragging. She followed the man home before she called Tony. He had lectured her about how dangerous it was for an untrained person to do police work."

Never once did the she reveal she had been an FBI agent. Now Tony sat embarrassed as he learned of her background. He chose to remain silent about his encounter with her. He, Boo and Dean had long since become friends.

Boo Jordan wrote books, some of the titles made Tony shake his head. *You Don't Have to Age, Who is the Old Lady in the Mirror* and *Yes, Men Can Learn To Be Sensitive.* Tony did not intend to put them on his reading list.

"You should." Ben and Juan said in unison.

"Want to pay her a visit?"

"Yes, I want her as the psychiatrist on this case. No one is more qualified," Ben said.

"We better get clearance from the boss." Juan joined the other two. "I'll call from the car."

Their superiors thought it a great idea. They weren't convinced anyone could get her to cooperate. After the attack, Boo turned in her badge, retired and moved to the Ozarks with her husband.

Within fifteen minutes, Tony turned his cruiser into the driveway leading up to a modest farmhouse. A man came out of the barn to the south and walked toward them.

"That's Dean, Dr. Jordan's husband," Tony said.

"Well, Sheriff, what can I do for you today? Do you have news about Courtney?"

"Yes, she's gained two pounds. Her parents will be here later today. Is Boo around? These men are from the FBI and would like to talk to her."

"She's in her office at the back of the house. Go on around." Dean pointed the way.

Tony knocked on the door of what looked like a converted sun porch.

"Come in." Her voice always made Tony smile. It sounded light and sparkly like someone waved a magic wand and her words floated of it.

The sheriff opened the door and stepped back to let the other two men go first. Dr. Jordan sat behind a small desk in a room surrounded by cases of books and magazines. The walls had photographs of her and Dean at several locations around the globe. In each one, they smiled at one another and held hands.

She looked up, raised a finger in a "hold on a minute gesture" and went back to her work. "I need about two minutes to finish my thought and then I'll be with you gentlemen. Please, have a seat."

The porch, turned office, had different seating areas separated by furniture and patterned rugs. The space around the desk looked professional with her on one side and three sturdy chairs facing it from the other side. Over near the windows a wicker settee, rocker and lounge chair sat facing a window. The men chose to sit there.

True to her word, Boo finished, shut down her computer and walked over. "Well, Ben Goodman, I haven't seen you in years. And I'm sorry; I don't remember your name." She nodded toward Juan. "And Tony, dear Tony. What can I do for you men?"

Juan reminded her of his name. She backed up to the coffee table behind her and perched on the edge. She said nothing

Ben spoke up. "We would like to have you work with the children of the recent tragedy on Cherokee Ridge."

Tony watched, as Boo appeared to study their faces. He looked her in the eye when she turned to him. "I'm retired," she said.

"I appreciate that. I guarantee you won't come into contact with a suspect in this case. They're long gone. They know we have their identities and they're running as fast as they can in the other direction." As Boo talked to Ben, she made her way to the window.

"That doesn't negate the fact that I am retired."

Tony remained seated to give her some space. Ben stood but stayed near his chair. "Boo. I was there that day. I know what happened to you, and I'm sorry. However, these children have spent from a few weeks to several months outside, chained to boxes, eating gruel. They need reassurance they are safe. We also need help reuniting them with their families."

Tony took over. "I interviewed each of them at the hospital and they say they don't want to go home. Seems every day Cletus Compton threatened them. Told them if they ever went home without his permission, he would come after them and kill their entire families. They knew, from what he did to them daily, that he told the truth. Some don't want to take a chance of even seeing their families in case he finds out."

Dr. Jordan turned to face the trio. "I'm sorry, Ben. Even if I wanted to, Dean would never stand for it. You have to understand what he went through. They told him, no less than five times, I wouldn't make it.

"I'm not so sure the Compton boys won't come back. They know the children saw everything they did. As I see it, you have two choices. Chase them down or lure them back. We all know which one would be the most effective. It's been over ten years since I pried into the mind of a killer."

She walked back to her desk, seemed to have

changed her mind and went to the door. She whistled, then motioned for someone, probably Dean, to come to join them.

Tony began to fill her in on some details. "There were seven children on the hill when the Comptons set it on fire. One died at the scene. It's one more thing the children need help to work through. Of course, there's Courtney. She's getting stronger, but has nightmares every night and is afraid to see her parents because she believes she disappointed them by not screaming like they always told her to do."

Dean came in. He went straight to his wife and put a protective arm around her. They were a striking couple. Dean stood straight and tall. The muscles twitched in his arms and his denim jeans strained against his thighs. His face, wrinkled from wind, and weather only made him appear more rugged.

Dr. Boo Jordan fit comfortably under his arm. She too was thin and muscular. Her hair gleamed in the sunlight. It underscored the gray that ran through it like ribbons. "Dean, these men want me to come out of retirement and be the psychological crutch for the children who were held captive on the mountain."

"And what was your answer?" He turned to look her in the eye. If he had an opinion, Tony couldn't tell by the look on his face. It emitted love and respect.

"I haven't given them one. They gave me their word, the suspects are in another part of the country and their only reason to come back here would be intimidate or get rid of the witnesses.""

"We both know this is where the witnesses are. How many children are there?" Her husband asked.

"Seven, including Courtney."

Tony explained the plan. "We rented Moccasin Boy Scout Camp. We'll move them there. You could work with them however you like, one on one, in a group, by age. You're the expert."

Juan, who sat quietly until now, spoke up. "We'll get you nurses, cooks, guards and any other support staff you want or need."

Ben's cell phone rang. He looked down at it and said, "Excuse me, I have to take this," as he walked out the door.

In a couple of minutes, he came back and joined the group. His face ashen, his voice shaky. "They have found bodies on the Ridge. Three so far. He turned toward Boo. "I wish you would think this over. I can get a psychologist from the Agency, but it wouldn't be the same." Tony and Juan were already at the door.

"I would like to go with you now." She patted Dean's arm.

"I'll drive you myself, if you don't mind. I don't want you stuck up there until all hours." Dean moved his hand down to her waist to escort her.

"Sure, that would be fine." Tony left. The Jordan's remained in the room.

Since the sheriff's office lay between Boo's farm and Cherokee Ridge, they went by there so the agents could pick up another car. Tony's stomach churned. This case got worse every day. In his career, he had only one other case involving kids.

A young father lost his two toddlers in a custody battle. Two days later, he stole them from the baby sitter at his ex-wife's house. He drove them to Table Rock Lake, rented a boat and once in the center of the lake, he threw them in and drown them. Later he killed himself. It had been five years. Tony thought about those kids, their grief stricken mother and deranged dad every day.

There were a hundred or more hopeful parents in his county now. They prayed one of the seven remaining children belonged to them. They came from all over the country. These parents had given up hope of finding their children again. Much like the tomb or the Unknown Soldier, one of these kids could be theirs until they heard differently.

The authorities had no way of knowing how many children these lunatics took over the years. The sheriff felt sure the exact number would remain a mystery. The only people who knew what happened were the victims and the men who took them.

Tony lost all track of time, buried in his own thoughts of more dead children. He pulled in behind Agent Goodman's SUV and got out. Juan lifted the crime scene tape over his head and held it while Tony and Ben scooted under. Before them lay three small body bags.

Two men were hard at work on another grave. One knelt with his knee in a shallow hole. The other brushed dirt off a skeleton. Another gruesome scene that would not fade with time.

Dr. Samuel Lambs, the medical examiner, borrowed from Buzzard County, supervised, but stopped to address the three newcomers. "Whoever buried these kids was meticulous. The graves are shallow, yet before he covered them with dirt, he took the time to put a board with their name, age and date of death on top of each one. He added small rocks all over the bodies to ward off wild animals. It's difficult to tell how many graves are here. If I go by the small mounds every three feet or so, I would say more than twenty."

Boo and Dean arrived in time to hear Dr. Lamb's estimation.

"Dr. Jordan, good to see you. Have you signed on to work with us? We could use all the help we can get," Dr. Lamb asked.

Tony shook his head. Did everyone know about Dr. Jordan's, past? Everyone but him?

"I'm not sure. I would love to work with the children. You know, try to get them started on the right path back to a normal life. The Jordans stepped closer to the body bags. "Are they all children?"

"Yes. Someone buried them in chronological order. The bodies we are finding now have newer dates. Looks like the cemetery goes toward the north, and we will find older ones. All bodies face east. Whoever dug these graves and buried the children cared enough about them to want them to face the morning sun."

"Why is that, Dr. Lamb, do you know?" Juan asked.

"The Christians foresee Jesus will come from the east at the second coming and the Jews always approach God from the east in the Tabernacle. It goes on and on."

"It doesn't go with the profiles of the men we're searching for. There's no indication they believe in anything," Juan said.

"We don't have much on Warren. He might be the gentle one. Perhaps he doesn't want to anger the gods or it might be something he learned in childhood. Hard to tell. Some of the children told me he took them for walks, fed them extra food, including fruits and carrots. He let them bathe in the creek when he and the boy were alone up there." Tony hated to say too much in front of Dean. With each statement, he glanced at the man to see his reaction. Dean remained quiet and calm. His expression never changed.

The group left at dusk and drove their separate ways down the mountain, agreeing to meet at the Boy Scout camp at noon the next day. Tony would try to have the key personal hired or at least some candidates in mind.

Dr. Boo Jordan never agreed to help, but she moved ahead with them as they made plans.

Boo told them having all the children together as they readjusted would make it easier on them. As the parents arrived, they could join their child at the camp. However, she didn't want the siblings around at this time; she feared it would be too much stress for the kids. "Small steps toward normal life," she said. "Seeing and dealing with the emotions of their parents is enough for now."

The other pluses included privacy and confidentiality. The hordes of people around the sheriff's office increased daily and had taken on a circus –like atmosphere, with food vendors, tee shirt sales and hawkers of every kind.

Tony made them all register and buy permits to try to keep the numbers down. The red tape might be a nuisance for them, but they kept coming.

The news media grabbed on to every bit of information they could get. The latest news of the graves on Cherokee Ridge would spread new angst through the masses.

Statistics said 800,000 children went missing in the United States every year, two thousand a day. Only 115 a year are stranger abductions. It occurred to Tony that the Compton brothers were responsible for a large number of those over the years.

CHAPTER NINE

The brothers were within five miles of their mama's place when they realized there were cops everywhere. Well, what did Cletus expect? Someone had to put an end to the Compton brothers.

Cletus became more belligerent with each passing minute. Warren smelled danger, he always could. Something hung in the air when he came close peril. Big brother laughed it off, but it never failed him.

Now what?

The visit with Mama would have to wait. Cletus turned the Lincoln around and headed toward Mobile. On the way, he drove to a big box store and told Warren to wait in the car with the motor running. "What are you going to do?"

"Do as I say, or there'll be just one of us going

to see Mama." Threats. Always threats as a means of control. The tactic him weary.

When his brother left, he slid over to the driver's seat and waited. Time passed slowly. It seemed like hours before Cletus came back. "Let's go. Drive out of the parking lot, go left and then right at the first stop light."

"Where are we going?" Warren never understood his brother's temperament or mentality, yet he followed his direction.

"Damned if I know. Just drive."

Why did he have to act the way he did? Warren followed directions. He drove until his brother told him to pull over.

Cletus took a smart phone from his shirt pocket and dialed a number. "Hi, Mama. It's me."

Warren couldn't hear much of his mother's side of the conversation. However, it became apparent her oldest son disagreed with what she had to say. He grunted into the phone and never answered her or spoke more than a word or two. When he hung up, he took the phone and stepped out of the car, dropped it on the sidewalk and jumped on it. He picked up all the pieces, put them in his pocket, sat back in the passenger seat and yelled, "Drive!"

"Where to?"

"Where I tell you, moron." Warren hated name-calling. He seethed between clinched teeth, but stayed silent. He drove until they were in the suburbs of Mobile. Each mile they drove put them further from Mama. The farther away he got from her, the calmer he felt and the nastier Cletus' mood.

For almost three hours after Cletus' rude

comments, the bothers rode in silence. "Pull over." The order came with a punch to his shoulder. Warren pulled over in front of a mailbox and watched while his brother got out, emptied the broken phone parts into the mail slot and slipped back into the car. "I'm hungry. Let's get some breakfast." Typical.

Warren had a flashback of Cletus eating the hamburger of the man he killed in Hardy only the day before and shivered. "Are you going to tell me what Mama said?"

"I said I'm hungry. I'll tell you while we eat." Earlier, he put his gun in the glove compartment. Now he retrieved it. Before he stuck the weapon into the waistband of his trousers, he rubbed it on his younger brother's face and neck. Warren slapped him away.

He tipped his head back and laughed.

In the south, there is a café on every corner. They picked one with only a few cars in the parking lot, went in and each a ordered the He-Man plater. Cletus told him their mama said there were police everywhere, on the roof next door, in a van outside, on a boat in the bayou and places she could not readily see. She asked why we never robbed liquor stores, people on the street, random houses, anything but banks and kidnapping, the two main crimes the FBI take an interest in and actively pursued.

Mama said she saw a wanted dead or alive poster of her precious boys on a bulletin board in the grocery store.

"Makes me want to take as many cops with me

as I can." He slapped his hand on the table. The noise echoed and the people in the restaurant looked toward them.

Warren said nothing more. He wished his brother would stop. Or that he had the guts to kill him, walk away and pretend none of this happened.

Cletus sat with his back to the counter. He sat facing it. A breaking new report flashed on a television screen above the counter. The place had cleared out. Only three people remained. There, displayed for them to see, was his driver's license photo and a composite sketch of Cletus scrolling across the bottom of the screen. Anyone could tell the faces on TV and the faces of the men in the booth by the window were one in the same.

He read it silently as it flowed past.

Cletus Beaufort Compton, age 42 and Warren Moss Compton, age 35. Wanted in Missouri for kidnapping, murder, car theft and arson. Wanted in Arkansas for murder. It is presumed they are heading south in a 2011 Lincoln, with Arkansas license plate- SAC 182. The men are armed and dangerous. If you see these men, do not confront them. Call 911 or the FBI hotline at 1-899-555-1212. There is a reward for any information leading to their arrest.

Warren looked around. The cook fried eggs for a man at the counter. The server gingerly wiped tables, straightened salt, peppershakers and catsup bottles as she went.

No one paid attention to the news. Warren leaned over to his brother and told him what he saw. He put his head back and laughed the same hideous laugh he used to make fun of Warren earlier. The three people in the café, who had paid no attention to them, now stared straight in their direction with fear and recognition. Warren realized the three folks had seen the report before and knew who they were.

The people looked away, but not before he caught their eye. Without hesitation, Cletus reached back and pulled out the forty-five.

"Let's just go. They didn't see anything."

"Little brother, can we take that chance?"

"I don't want any more blood on my hands. Slide out of the booth and walk to the car like nothing's wrong. I'll leave enough money on the table for the bill and the tip. Please!"

"Please." Cletus mocked in a high-pitched sissy voice. "You go first. I'll pay the bill. That way I'll be able to tell if they recognized us. Go ahead, start the car. Drive up to the door."

Warren shrugged his shoulders, took a deep breath and ran out of the restaurant, jumped in the car and revved the engine. "God, give me the strength to drive away." Then he began to cry. He knew all too well God wouldn't listen to him now.

He heard the shots. They sounded like firecrackers. One for the cook, one for the customer at the counter and another for the young server. Cletus came out with a maniacal grin on his face. "Now we won't have to worry about who saw what," he said. "Let's get rid of this car and head back to Atlanta."

The two cities were four and a half hours apart. They had been back and forth twice in two days. Warren felt a primal scream build inside him.

On command, he drove to a ritzy subdivision, and cruised around to find the perfect house to steal a car. Cletus had two criteria. The dwelling had to be empty and not have an alarm sign on the house or in the yard. Three hours later, they found the perfect place. Warren jimmied the lock on the front door. The brothers walked through the house to the garage. On their way they picked up all the keys on a rack. One bay was empty; in the other, one sat a new Lexus with less than a thousand miles on it. Although it would be equipped with the latest antitheft software, Cletus wanted it.

Warren put the car they had been driving in the garage and poured two bottles of bleach, they found in the house, all over the inside of it. They took the other car and left.

Forty miles away, they stole the plates off a Jaguar in long term parking on the top floor of a pubic garage, put them on the Lexus and headed back toward Mama's.

At a Wal-Mart store in Montgomery, they stopped for a change of clothes and more hair dye. The colors they chose last week were so different from their natural hair they looked funky now. When they escaped from Cherokee Ridge, they left all their personal belonging. Cletus didn't want them to have anything to keep track of but the money. It forced them to stop and buy new clothes and underwear every time they wanted to clean up.

Nothing bothered Cletus' appetite and since he never finished his breakfast back at the diner, he loaded the cart with food he could eat cold or warm in a microwave.

They stopped for the night. Warren went to the office and checked them in while his brother parked the car in a space facing away from the room.

The next morning, Cletus dyed his hair strawberry blond, and had Warren shave his head so it stood up no more than an inch all over. He looked like a military recruit in his first week of boot camp. Warren left his hair longer, but dyed it what the bottle called warm brown.

Cletus told him the plan he devised to get near their mother. "I'm gonna leave you at Matthew's Fishing Lodge on the Flint River. I'll leave you half of the money. If I'm not back in two days, rent a boat and go to the Jackson Airport where the runways cross over the river. You can't miss it. Do as I say, because if I don't come back, you're on your own." Cletus always talked to his younger brother as if he couldn't understand the simplest sentence. "Remember, if you don't rent a boat, you'll have to steal your transportation. No one will sell you anything with the ten year old driver's license you carry."

"Why don't I just go with you?"

"Because they are looking for two men. Besides, I want to see Mama by myself. You and her weren't close." He walked to the trunk of the Lexus, took one of the bags of money and tossed it to Warren. "No use the feds ending up with all of it. Now let's go before I do shoot you."

CHAPTER TEN

Exhuming the bodies on Cherokee Ridge turned out to be a slow, tedious job. They found twenty-two children. It took eight days.

Some had tree roots weaving and wandering through their skeletons, others had been there so long they removed them one bone at a time.

The forensic team took pictures of each grave. The bones were marked and put in body bags. Any clothing, hair, barrettes or jewelry, ended up in a separate bag with the same number as the corresponding body. The place remained ghostly quiet, not even gallows humor seemed appropriate.

Boo and Dean showed up on the top of the ridge several times during the week. Juan, Ben and Tony went back as much as they could. Tony felt helpless up there. He could only watch and note the growing body count.

Reports about the Comptons and their exploits came in daily.

Two men answering their descriptions stole cars, broke into houses and shot three people at a small diner in a Mobile suburb. A young server survived to tell her story. She lay in critical condition at an undisclosed hospital under armed guard, in case the brothers came back to finish her off.

Tony and Cara moved the center of their operation to Camp Moccasin where they could keep an eye on the children. Sixteen days after the killing fire on the Ridge and the Compton boys still ran free.

The children would be in residence at the camp by Thursday evening, except for Courtney whose mother insisted she would take her home as soon as they packed.

Courtney did not want to go with her mother. She knew if she did, the bad men would come and hurt her family. Tony and Boo met with them at the Sheriff's office to try to persuade the worried mother, her daughter would be better off, in the end, if she stayed.

Tony had Cara take the little girl for a soda while the three adults talked. Tony had never heard Boo use a stern voice.

"Mrs. Hamilton, I understand your desire to take Courtney home. However, under the circumstances, it isn't a good idea."

"The doctor assures me my little girl is strong and healthy and will not suffer any lasting effects from her ordeal."

"And I whole heartedly agree. Physically, your daughter will be fine. The sheriff and I are concerned with her long-term mental health. The man who adducted these children tormented them daily. One of the techniques he used was fear. Children, anyone for that matter, are easier to control if they are scared. The other staple in a child's life is her family. He threatened to kill your family if she went home without his permission. Until these men are apprehended, the children do not feel safe."

Tony said nothing, but he shook his head in agreement.

"Are you telling me I am not allowed to take my child with me?"

Boo shook her head. "I am telling you that I believe these men will be in custody soon. If you and Courtney go along with our plans to house the children all in one place to make them feel safe until they are mentally stable enough to go home, she will have a much shorter adjustment period." For a long moment, the office was quiet.

"Fine. I want to do what is best for my baby. I do want it noted, however, that I do not approve of your tactics."

"And I can appreciate that Mrs. Hamilton. Thanks for your cooperation."

Cara brought Courtney back to her mother. When she found out she could stay, she ran to Boo and hugged her. Mrs. Hamilton merely shook her head.

The FBI had field agents at the main camp entrance. One road came into the camp, meandered around the grounds and went back out. To come in from the back or the sides would take both daylight and hiking skills. All paths led to a central clearing in front of the main building, where during camping season, the Boy Scouts raised and lowered the flag.

Tony had guards on the highest points of the campgrounds where they could watch the cabins and paths. They worked in pairs, one deputy and one highway patrol officer. Every four hours they changed vantage points. Every eight hours they changed shifts.

Tony took a lot of time to work out a plan. He sat down with Ben and Juan and they agreed no one could get near the camp without detection. They had the definite advantage if the Comptons chose to come back. Tony had a small twinge of guilt knowing even if they told Boo the brothers would not return to the area. He hoped they would.

Boo wanted to meet with all the parents and the families, before she met with the child victims. The meeting took place on Friday morning in the cafeteria. Tony, Juan and Ben sat in on the talk.

"Hello everyone. I am Dr. Boo Jordan. I am a trained FBI agent and a psychiatrist. I know you have many questions. If you let me talk, I can answer most of them. If I don't, you are free to ask anything you like, when I am finished."

Cara walked around and served hot coffee to the parents. Once everyone settled down, Boo began. "We are here today because your children survived a horrendous ordeal. Let me begin by pointing out that kidnapping is child abuse. Your child underwent a grotesque transition from being one of the most important people in someone's life to a situation where a stranger had complete and absolute power over them.

"This ordeal is even more traumatic for a child because they are used to being taken care of. The first thing we need to address is whether the kids will be normal again. I say, yes, but they will have to reintegrate into their families at their own pace. Some of them might be ready to go home in a week, others, might take longer. They have a form of the Stockholm syndrome, a psychological condition in which they formed an attachment to their captures. In the case of your children, they are afraid to go home because Cletus forbid it. This man swore he would kill the entire family if they went home without his permission. They take that statement as literal truth and are willing to stay away forever to keep you all safe."

Questions went on for an hour. In the end, they agreed to let the kids meet with Boo as long as necessary. It would be a struggle for most of them. No one lived in Missouri. Cletus took his victims from at least two or three states away. The parents had jobs, other children and lives back home. On the other hand, they wanted their child happy, safe and healthy and were willing to do whatever it took to make it happen.

The rest of the weekend, the families could spend time to reacquaint themselves with their child. On Monday morning, sessions with Dr. Jordan began.

Tony had Cara look after the parents needs and put them in the small cabins.

The sheriff took the time to go to each cabin and talk to the family assigned to it. He started with Austin's parents. "Please do not go out on the grounds alone. You're not prisoners, by any means, and we do not expect for the men responsible for all of this to come back to this area but we are taking no chances. The grounds are heavily guarded. You are free to go between the cabins, to the mess hall and the recreation room. Thanks for your cooperation."

Austin's dad, Bryon asked. "Should we prepare ourselves for a boy we no longer know?"

Tony took time to consider the question. "No, I don't. I interviewed your son in the hospital after the fire. He has seen horrors most adults couldn't handle. One of the kids fell off the ridge and died in front of him. Cletus Compton scared the beegeebees out of him daily. However, he will come around, maybe sooner than we realize. There is a lot to be said for family love."

Ben, Juan and Tony rode into town for a press conference. Ben did the talking. "Ladies and gentlemen, to keep hearsay to a minimum and to make sure the facts released to the public are accurate, we have some new information for you. The FBI team and the CSI Major Case Squad from Lindell, found twenty-two bodies on Cherokee Ridge. They are all children. Identifying them could take some time.

"Whoever buried these children wrote their identity on an object and left it on top of each body. We don't know if it is accurate, but it is a starting place." Ben shifted his weight from one foot to another. "I anticipate one of your first questions will be to ask about the object we found with each child. We will not release those details at this time. Including the child who died at the scene of the fire, it brings the total to twenty-three deceased. Seven children survived, but we have no idea how many were kidnapped and reunited with their families over the years.

"We realize some people paid the ransom and never contacted the police, out of fear. People's memories of the fine details fade over the years. Clues, if there were any, are long gone."

One reporter shouted out a question. Ben raised his arm and signaled for quiet.

"The first child, the one found on Bear Road, and the six children who survived the fire, will be moved to an undisclosed location. They will be debriefed, checked by a psychiatrist and a medical doctor a few more times before they are free to go home."

Media personalities, from TV, newspaper and radio, began to shout questions to the three. Tony took a step closer to the microphone. "Because the victims are minors, we are limited to the amount and type of information we can release. You will have to trust us that when more facts become available, we will pass them along. Again, we thank you for your time and patience."

All three men turned toward the courthouse and walked away.

CHAPTER ELEVEN

Most of the people in the area knew Boo Jordan as a famous author. Everyone knew she had been a practicing psychiatrist, however no one knew her as a retired and decorated FBI agent.

Boo felt bad because some of the parents had been in town for two weeks, hoping to get information about their children who had been missing for years. The first couple she spoke to was the Baxters.

"Mr. and Mrs. Baxter, I am Dr. Jordan. I want to talk to you about your son, Boyd. According to the FBI reports, Boyd went missing on August 1, 1999 from a shopping mall where you and he were having lunch in the food court?"

Mrs. Baxter began to tear up. "That is correct."

"Boyd's body was found in a burned out cabin on Cherokee Ridge the day of the fire." Boo knew it was best to tell bad news without a flourish of words.

The lady gasped and put her hand to her mouth. "Oh, my God, he's been alive all these years, and now he's gone again. Really gone!"

When Mrs. Baxter started to sob, Mr. Baxter put his arm around his wife's shoulder and looked at Boo. "Boyd was three when he went missing. Why would the kidnappers keep him?"

"It is referred to at the Stockholm Syndrome. The child forms a bond with his captor. In Boyd's case, his affliction would contribute to that scenario."

"We were told that with proper care and stimulation, he could advance."

"Unfortunately, we will never know." Boo leaned over and put a hand on Ethel Baxter's knee. "I want you to know, there was nothing you could have done differently to prevent this."

"But he was only three when they took him. To know he lived to be a young man without us breaks my heart."

"I know. The FBI is prepared to have Boyd's body transported to Toledo for you."

"Thank you for telling us about our boy," Wilber said. "We have looked in every crowd for seventeen years wondering if one of those kids was Boyd. The entire family will sleep better knowing where he is and where he has been."

One down, twenty-eight more to go.

Boo met eleven-year-old Austin Murray. It would be the first of many similar conversations she would have with scared kids in the next few weeks.

"Hi Austin. I'm Dr. Jordan, Boo Jordan. I know it will be difficult, but I would like to talk to you about your kidnapping. I want to know everything you remember about the men, the place you lived, all of it. Are you up to that?"

They were in a small office where the director of the camp usually worked. Boo had all sorts of food and drink and toys brought in to make the children more comfortable. It looked like a sports store with every kind of ball, racket and helmet she could find. She had a big metal bucket filled with ice and cold drinks. Her personal favorite, chocolate Yahoo chilled with the others. There were snack cakes, donuts, fresh fruit and candy.

Austin sat straight in his chair. "Is your name really Boo?"

She laughed. "Unfortunately, yes."

"Jeez, who would do that to a kid?"

"My mother. There were seven of us. She named us Echo, Boo, Halo, Ocean, Island, Sand and Robert."

"Robert?" Austin grinned. "Why Robert?"

"She wanted to name one of us after her father."

She saw Austin relax in his chair. "Is that a true story, Dr. Jordan?"

"Yes, do you want to hear something even more bizarre?"

"Sure, what?"

"My brother Robert goes by Buddy."

They both laughed. In the days that followed, she told the story six more times. When she repeated the tale, it sounded as if she'd shared it for the first time.

Each of these children were precious to her and they had all been through hell. She wanted them to know they could relax now.

Austin told her the same thing he told Tony about the day of his kidnapping. Only with Boo, he added the feelings of fear and anxiety. He spent a lot of time on how guilty he felt for not paying attention to his surroundings. He worried everyday about what his abduction did to his parents. He fretted over his little sister, knowing she would never have a normal life. He knew his mom and dad would never again let her out of their sight.

"I wish I could just go home and act like it never happened," Austin said.

"You can, to a point. The less you talk about it to people, the quicker the minute details will fade. Do you want a cold drink?" Boo got up to grab a drink and tossed him one.

"My mom and dad have a million questions. It's so bad I hate to see them. Do they know it would be better if I didn't talk about it?"

"I will tell them. I will also ask them to find you a therapist in case you do want to talk. Best to tell your stories to someone who can handle them." Boo took a drink of her chocolate soda. "I love this."

"It's good, but it's been so long since I had anything that tastes good, everything is too sweet."

"One more question." She looked the boy in the eyes. "If I talk to your parents and little sister, let them know you should open up about this at your own pace, would you like to go home?"

"Sure, when?"

"In a day or two. You are a wise young man, Austin. I want to warn you about something else. All of your old friends will seem young and foolish to you. What they deem important, what you used to consider important, will diminish and seem silly to you now.

"These men, in many ways, took your childhood from you. At least the part where your parents did the worrying and you played. You will have to be patient with all of them. Do you understand?"

"Yes. How long will my friends be the way they are? Will I ever fit in again?"

"Sure, but it might take a while. I remember the day I realized bad things can happen in life." Boo knew how to relate but the stories she told were true.

"Will you tell me about it, Dr. Jordan?"

"Of course. My mom, dad, aunt, uncle and brother were mushroom hunting in the woods near Stockton Lake. My sister drove up, jumped out of the car and began to cry. Seems my Grandfather died while taking cattle to market. I watched Mom, Dad, and my brother Michael leave with my sister and head to Grandma's." She sat her drink down, she liked to move her hands when she talked. "I wondered why I didn't get to go. They took my brother and only eighteen months separated us in age. Nevertheless, they left me behind with my aunt and uncle. At age nine, I had limited understanding of the gravity of the situation. Their abandonment, at least what I felt was abandonment at the time, is what I will never forget. It seemed an eternity before I saw them again. When I did, they were sad and crying. Grandma almost ignored me when I went in the house. I never felt so alone."

"I feel alone. I could never tell my story aloud. It would sound like a bad horror movie." Austin stretched his long legs out in front of him. "Go ahead, Dr. Jordan."

"Well, in the country they sometimes put the body in the parlor for viewing. They did that with Grampa. My sister and I slept in the bedroom behind the wall where he lay. People said he looked natural, but he looked anything but like himself to me. He never slept with his glasses on, and in real life he smiled and laughed all the time. I hung around in the room with his body and stood close to the casket and stared at him. I even touched him. His skin felt cold and waxy. To this day, dead bodies look dead to me." Boo put one hand on each of her knees and waited.

"I didn't think I would ever be able to sleep again." Austin put his hands on his opposite arms as if he had a chill. "Did it make your friends seem different?"

"No, but I was different. In the back of my mind, I knew bad would and could happen. I never knew it before that day. The same thing will happen to you. You will catch a baseball and for the first time in your life, realize you could have missed and have it hit you in the face."

"Jeez." The young man sunk down in his chair.

"Don't get me wrong, it won't last. You will be happy again. I am trying to let you know you will be more aware of unimportant events. It might last a month, a year, or the rest of your life. Don't let it stop you from being who you are meant to be. Never let fear keep you from doing anything. Remember, you will get stronger every day. We've covered everything. I'm sure you're tired. Oh my goodness, we talked longer than I realized. You will be late for dinner."

"I'm surprised talking made me feel better." The boy stood.

"I'm glad our visit helped you. You can talk to me any time. Even after you get home, you can still call."

Boo stood to walk the boy to the door, but instead of going toward it, he took a step toward her and hugged her. She hugged him back. He began to cry. She held him until he finished and let her go on his own.

CHAPTER TWELVE

Tony Massey never wanted to be famous and he never thought a small place like Ash County would make the national news cycle. However, the story of the dead children and the Compton brothers captured the imagination and macabre side of the public's attention.

More disgusting details came out every day. Dead children, burned bodies, the Comptons on a crime spree that rivaled the old mafia wars in Chicago years ago.

People mentioned them, and Bonnie and Clyde Barrow in the same breath. Everyday someone called and wanted to do an expose featuring him and Ash County. Others wanted secret details so they could write true crime stories or scoop the big networks.

Tony no longer answered his phone. More and

more he avoided people. Before this happened, he loved his job. As long as he could remember, he wanted to be a police officer or a sheriff. The favorite television programs of his youth were NYPD Blue, Walker, Texas Ranger, and Law and Order.

At age sixteen, he directed traffic at the Ash County Fair. On those occasions, he wore a Junior Deputy badge. People described him as earnest. He had a growing spurt in junior high and shot up to six feet six that summer.

Tony spent a lot of time at Camp Moccasin in his youth. He camped there with his Boy Scout Troop. Later he went through the Eagle Scout's ceremony in the same area the flagpoles stood. When he came home summers from college, he worked there as a camp counselor.

The career he pictured mimicked a Norman Rockwell painting straight off the cover of The Saturday Evening Post. Never, when he daydreamed about his life, did he include murder and kidnapping in the mysteries he would solve.

He sat high on a hill overlooking the main lodge at the camp. It gave him a chance to get away from the news people, the phones and the noise. The realization that the Comptons were no closer to capture than they were twenty-one days ago, kept him awake at night.

A dry branch snapped behind him. In one smooth and fluid motion, he drew his gun, laid down and rolled over so he could see what or who stood behind him.

"Wait, wait," someone said. Ben Goodman

stepped into the clearing and waved his arms.

"Are you trying to get yourself killed?" Tony sat up and holstered his weapon.

"I hope not, not on this beautiful day. I came to talk to you." Ben squatted next to Tony.

"Somebody else die down there today?" Tony tried to stay out of the spotlight.

"No, but I have an idea. Since this is your county, your camp and your people, I thought I'd run an idea by you before I go any further with it."

"Okay," Tony said. "You're going to carry out a plan whether I like it or not, but you want me to know about it anyway."

"Yeah, that's about it. People are shooting each other in the streets of Atlanta and Mobile. If they spot someone resembling the fugitives, or anyone who fits their description they shoot first and find out later they shot the neighbor's son-in-law or the noise they heard out the bedroom window turned out to be the neighbor's beloved cat. Get my drift?"

"Sure, I know what you're saying. What's the plan?"

"It isn't my plan. I'll let the director take all the credit."

"Okay, don't let my imagination run wild. What do you want to do?"

Ben looked down. If the plan had any merit, Ben would implement it, and not come to him to sugar coat it.

"The director wants us to leak lies about the brothers."

"What kind of lies?" Tony shook his head when he heard the plan.

"That the children were beaten. That Cletus took the children to prove his manhood. He held them prisoner so he had someone beneath him. That he didn't rape them because he is impotent."

"Ben, is the FBI prepared to get us all killed? Does Boo know you want to lure those lunatics back here with the hopes of capturing them? I was there when you promised her she and the bad guys would never meet."

"No, she doesn't. Juan and the director want you to be there when we lay out the plan for her. And to Dean, of course."

"What's the last report on the Comptons?"

"Cletus tried to visit his mother at her home on the Black Bayou over a week ago. Twenty law enforcement officers hid within two miles and yet he escaped. To hear their story, he disappeared into thin air. No one has seen him since. Maybe they wounded him. They found the car a block from the house. No one saw Warren. We don't know if they split up or if one of them is hurt or dead."

"I thought the FBI always got their man." Tony sounded serious.

"I don't blame you for being upset, but we can't let this go on forever. We can try to lure them back here where we have the advantage. You know the land, and the people. We can protect Dr. Jordan and her husband, if necessary. We'll get the kids out of here before we start. Boo said they could all go home within a day or two. We can hold off that long."

"What if they go after the children?" Tony liked the idea less the more he heard.

"They won't. The children are all over the country. We'll keep them under armed guard until we apprehend the brothers. I cleared it to have two men with each child twenty-four-seven until this is over. Come on, Tony, We need to put an end to this. If you have a better idea, now is the time to tell me."

"Just for the record, I don't like the idea. I hate the thought of them in Ash County. I hate the thought of them here, in this place. Although, I see the logic in it."

"So you will help me convince Boo to do it?"

"No Ben, I will help you present it to her. I won't give my opinion."

"That's more than I had thought I would get." Ben held out his hand to Tony. "Thanks."

"Don't thank me yet." Tony clinched his jaw.

Tony remained siting, so Ben sat beside him. "Where's Juan?"

"He went back to Tulsa for a couple of days. His boy, Jayce is in a play. He thought his wife would divorce him and the boy would never speak to him again if he missed every performance. Besides, there's enough paper work for him to do back there to keep him busy." Ben stretched his legs out in front of him.

"What about you? It's been a month for you too." Tony stalled. He thought it unfair to drag Boo into this any further when they all knew she almost died once before when she dealt with a criminal.

"My wife is supposed to come here for the weekend. That was before the director came up with the idea to bring the brothers here."

Tony stood, held his hand down to Ben to offer him an arm up. They headed toward Dr. Jordan's office; might as well get this over with. He remained quiet on the way down the hill. Mentally, he counted how many men he could get to guard everyone. They had cut down to one in each direction on the hills, two in the guard house at the entrance and one at each of the three buildings they were using. With the kids gone, they could bring in food. That would eliminate the kitchen; the two dorms they housed the kids in would be empty. That left only Boo to guard. Maybe he should suggest they let her go home and protect her there.

Boo sat at her desk with a legal pad and pen in her hand. It occurred to Tony she might be at work on her new book. If she thought it strange Ben and Tony came to see her, she kept quiet about it.

They went through the proper greetings before Ben laid the entire plan out for her. Occasionally she stopped him to ask a question. Most of the time, she sat and listened.

When Ben finished, he just said, "Well?"

Boo got out of her chair, walked to the window and looked out. "I guess this would be a good place to end it. We have the advantage because of the terrain. We would have more men. They could have the element of surprise, if they are smart enough. They will also have anger and indignation on their side. That shouldn't be taken lightly."

Ben sat down on the edge of her desk. "What do you mean?"

"Have you read any of my reports, Agent Goodman?"

"No ma'am, I haven't." His face turned crimson. "It isn't that I'm not interested. I'm on the other end of the case now. The end that is trying to catch them."

"Good enough, Agent. Let's have a seat over here and I will share some facts with you." She walked toward some lounge chairs pulled into a circle near the center of the room. "I know little about Warren. He tried to be kind to the children while they were on the Ridge. More to the point though, he still did as his brother's bidding. Cletus is the leader, the oldest and a truly evil man. Then again, only to a point."

Tony spoke for the first time. "I'm not sure what you are trying to say."

"Warren fed the children fruits and veggies when his brother wasn't around. He picked up the banana peelings, the orange peels and any scraps before his brother came back to camp. He took the children for walks, let them bathe in the creek on warm days and got them extra blankets on cold nights. Yet he rarely spoke to or went near the captives the days Cletus was there. He is afraid of his brother. I don't know why he is still with him."

Ben said, "Yes, but he snapped Boyd Baxter's neck."

"I didn't say he was a nice man. Only that he is not as far gone as Cletus. I don't think Warren likes to kill. Cletus enjoys it. This is why your plan will work, and why it scares the hell out of me." She crossed her arms as if there was a sudden chill in the room. "Cletus has some sense of fairness where these kids are concerned. He took the money from the parents and kept the kids for varying lengths of time. It had to do with how much trouble they caused him when it came time to pay the ransom. One little girl he took was so poor they were on Go Fund Me trying to raise the ransom. He ended up taking a thousand dollars and gave the girl back in three weeks.

"My point is this: He did not molest any children. He let them go at some point, and gave them money to get home. He took those kids hundreds of miles from their homes and let them out in high visibility areas. I have no idea what motivates him. I know if you add up all the children he kidnapped over the last fifteen years, and the ransoms he demanded, he has well over two million dollars."

"So why not leave the country?" Ben shook his head. "Why do it for so long, and take the chance someone would discover them up there. We found nothing of value on the Ridge. The truck was old. People said they dressed in rags, what where they were waiting for? It doesn't make sense to me."

Boo tried to explain, "You are putting societal rules on a psychopath. It can't be done. From my conversations with the victims and their parents, one motivation is to prove he is smarter than anyone else. Somewhere along the line someone made him feel inferior, and abused him. He sees the need to visit his mother. I suspect because everything has gone wrong. He needs to see her, to assure her it wasn't his fault. Most likely, he will blame the boy, Boyd. That's why they killed him. He can now justify that the fire, the men he killed, are all because Boyd screwed up. He is a mama's boy because he could never please her.

"I wouldn't be surprised if there was a sexual relationship there also. It is why he chose not to molest the children. He would see it as being disloyal to his mother. If you want to get him here, release these facts. Call him a mama's boy. Say he wasn't too smart and did his jobs the hard way. Mention that the FBI was only one-step behind him when the fire broke out. In addition, say he abused the kids sexually and physically. He will come back to set the record straight. I guarantee it."

"Would you do an exposé? One of those criminal profiles on both of them and let them know you're here. We don't want to draw this out any longer than possible."

"I need to talk to Dean. This will upset him. When I got injured in St. Louis, I gave this up. I promised I would die of old age sitting by the fire with my shawl over my shoulders. It will be hard on him to let this happen."

"What if he says, no?" Tony asked.

"Dean would never say no. We don't have that kind of relationship. However, I do intend to keep my promise and die of old age." Boo smiled the strangest smile Tony had ever seen.

"So let's concentrate on reuniting the children with their families. Get them home and guarded. Then you can write profiles of both of them. In it, can you blame everything on Cletus?" Tony could now see it would work. "But I have one more idea. Why don't I make all the statements about the men? As sheriff, I could give those facts and the media would listen."

"Thanks Tony for trying to protect me. It wouldn't seem credible coming from you. It needs to come from an FBI profiler or a doctor. We'll just leave out the 'retired' part."

CHAPTER THIRTEEN

Cletus parked the Lexus about five blocks from his childhood home and began to stroll through the old neighborhood. No one would recognize him with his blond hair and clean cut look.

He stopped when he got in sight of the house and lit a cigarette. He stood against a tree to smoke and survey the situation. Two men in dark copycat suits with bulges under the arm began to walk toward him. They came down the sidewalk, one from each direction.

He tensed; his entire body on alert. He opened his mouth, let the cigarette fall and began to run. He jumped a low privet hedge to his right, circled a black Ford Escape that sat near a huge maple tree and dropped out of sight. He ran through yards, down driveways, and always took the sparse path with less obstacles to slow him down.

Sirens wailed, dogs barked and people gawked. Cletus ran.

As luck would have it, he lost his sense of direction and sprinted toward the Black Bayou. It ran sixty-six miles down the Louisiana and Texas rivers, seven miles north of the city. He couldn't go into the swamp. It would be dark soon. If he went into uncharted waters at dusk, he knew he would die there.

The sirens now sounded from blocks behind him. No dogs or people were around. He stood behind a giant live oak to catch his breath. Then he climbed the tree. The thing towered over part of a common area and jogging path. It grew near the water along with four more the same size or bigger.

In late September in the Ozarks, the leaves would be sparse, but near Atlanta, the trees were still dressed. He looked up. The canopies of the oaks meshed together the further up he looked.

He knew if he could climb high enough, he would be safe.

Cletus scurried up the tree like someone half his age, and stopped where the tree on his left touched the one he climbed. It amazed him how big the limbs were that far up. For a minute, he wondered if he had picked the best hiding place.

Two joggers ran past and a police car drove by. He saw the number seven on the roof of the vehicle. The patrol car slowed down, then stopped. The officers were talking to the runners. They shook their heads no, to whatever questions the police asked. For the time being, he was safe.

Police cars, FBI black SUV's, unmarked cars

and officers on foot searched for hours. Thank goodness, no dogs joined them. Maybe he should throw something at them. They were so dumb. Nobody looked up. If it were the other way around, he would look in the trees. They needed to wise up if they intended to catch him.

At noon the next day, he was still in the tree. No one had searched for him in hours. They either had given up or went to search in another area. A few minutes later, he sat on a bus headed for Memphis with all sorts of stops in between.

* * * *

Warren stayed in his room most of the time, watching television, and napping.

His mind flashed from horror to horror all night. First, dead children haunted him, then the bodies of all those Cletus killed joined in. When he got the nerve to go for a walk, he prayed no one would recognize him.

The lodge where he had a room catered to anglers. Each room had a kitchen, bathroom and small deck in the back with a barbeque grill. Men gutted and filleted fish every hour of the day.

Warren wished he could be normal, live a life where he can fish and relax. Wouldn't happen now. He'd snapped Boyd's neck in front of a group of children; then went on the run with Cletus after his brother killed a man. At least he'd talked Cletus into letting him bury the bodies of the children who died on Cherokee Ridge.

Yes, he took the wrong path and couldn't go

back.

The newspaper, in a rack outside the convenience store, had a story about Cletus' narrow escape in Atlanta. Maybe he wouldn't come to get him. Warren began to make plans for what he could do on his own,

He would get more hair dye, spray tan, head for the airport, and fly to New York. From there, he would take remote paths and sneak into Canada. Once he got there, he would load up on a winter's worth of supplies, rent a cabin in the wilderness and stay put until spring. His gut told him that someone would kill Cletus soon. They would not look for him anymore. By summer, the news focus would be elsewhere.

Most of the men he saw paid no attention to the outside world. They fished, ate, drank beer, smoked cigars, and looked and smelled as if they never shaved or showered.

To have to run from the cops scared him. He saw no glory in dying or in a shootout with the police. Besides, he never owned a gun and his hunting knife wouldn't help him in a gunfight. Several times, he read about the knife he had strapped to his leg with a bandana, so he put the knife away in hopes it would make him harder to identify.

Every night he would wait until the middle of the dinner rush, order ahead and pick up the food when no one had time to notice him. The food at a beer joint near the marina tasted good to him.

At the far end of a river walk was the marina, a ten-minute stroll from the lodge. He went there morning, noon and night. The fast moving river mesmerized him; he stared at it for hours. It would be an easy out. If he jumped in he wouldn't have to worry about the police, FBI, nightmares, his own cowardice or his brother.

The water reflected the image of the trees, clouds, everything above it perfectly. The ripples and whirlpools enhanced the affect. For a minute or two, he relaxed and enjoyed his surroundings.

An unknown force propelled him toward the water's edge. Another two inches and he would be in the frigid whirlpool. No sound came when he tried to scream. Then the same power pulled him away from the edge and threw him on the sidewalk with such force his head bounced.

When the pain subsided, he opened his eyes. There stood Cletus. "What the hell are you doing? Are you trying to kill me?"

"Little brother, if I wanted to kill you, you'd be dead."

"How long have you been here?" He hoped Cletus hadn't heard him crying.

"Long enough, Whitey."

Warren rolled over on his stomach and used his hands and feet, then arms and legs to muscle himself off the pavement. "How'd you get here? I heard you were almost captured at Mama's."

"Almost doesn't count." He stretched his neck and looked around as if the scenery bored him.

Warren wanted to change the subject. "Are you hungry? I ordered some food from a bar down the street. I'm on my way to pick it up."

"Did you order enough for two? I doubt it."

Cletus slapped him on the ear as he did when they were kids. "We don't have time to eat anyway. We need to get out of here.'

"And go where?"

"Canada."

"You need a passport for that, I don't have one anymore."

"You never had one. Now go get your food and haul yourself back here. You can eat on the way."

The younger man no longer had an appetite, yet to argue with Cletus served no purpose but to anger him. He headed for the café. "What room are you in? Toss me the key."

"16."

"I'll meet you there."

Warren ran to get the food order and back to the lodge. The door to his room stood ajar. He pushed it open. Cletus sat on the bed covered in blood.

"Are you hurt?" The smell of fresh warm blood is distinct. Warren gagged.

He pointed out the door. "No, but he is!"

Warren tried not to look. Someone else's life ended at his brother's hand. Once on the deck, he looked around. A man lay stretched out, his legs toward the door. A police officer dead in a pool of blood.

This changed everything.

Cletus stepped out behind him. "If you're not going to eat, I will." He wiped his bloody hand down his pant leg, opened the box, took out a hand full of fries, and crunched on them. "Sure you don't want any?" He held the paper bag toward his brother.

Warren wretched again. Cletus laughed.

"Couldn't you at least wash your hands? What happened here?"

"A cop who fancied himself a hero. He walked behind me all the way down the river walk. I had to kill him."

"A cop! You had to kill a cop!"

Cletus put his head back and roared. "Do you believe it would go better for us if we didn't kill a cop? At this point, what possible difference could it make? His car is out front. We're going to drive it out of here."

"That's a bad idea." Warren shook his head.

Cletus put down the food and lunged at his brother. "I've 'bout had it with you. Get your gear. We're leaving. Now."

Ten minutes later, they drove away from the Flint River in the police cruiser. About fifty miles before they reached the Mississippi border, a young couple with car trouble waved them down. "This should be fun." Cletus winked as he got out of the car.

"Don't hurt them." Warren called after his brother.

"Don't hurt them." He mimicked and sauntered up to the kids. "What's wrong?"

"We're out of gas." The boy looked at Cletus and then to the car and finally at Warren.

Warren figured he would say something to anger Cletus and get himself killed. The young man pushed the girl, who stood next to him, behind him and tried to look a little taller. "Looks like you officers are off duty. We can figure out something else."

"Oh, no. We want to help, don't, we little brother?" He motioned for his brother to join him.

Warren watched the boy's knees buckle and knew he recognized them.

This could only get worse. "Let's go."

"And leave these kids stranded on a cold, lonely road?" Cletus pulled out the 45, moved behind the girl and ran the barrel up and down her cheek and neck. She screamed.

"It's okay, Janice, he's not a rapist, you'll be fine."

Cletus stepped around the girl and kicked the boy to the ground. "What's your name, boy?"

"Thomas." The boy had sense enough to stay down.

"Who are we, Thomas?" Cletus pointed to himself and then toward his brother.

"You're the Compton brothers."

"We're famous, Whitey."

"Infamous, is more like it. Let's get out of here. Those kids can't hurt us." Warren grabbed his arm and tried to pull him toward the patrol car.

"How do you know I don't rape women?" He prodded the boy with his foot.

Warren looked toward the kid and shook his head no. The boy's only chance was to shut up.

Cletus leaned down to Thomas and put the gun to the boy's temple. "Better tell what you know young man, before I count to three. One…"

"It was in today's paper. Some doctor, where you held those kids, told all about you."

"Like what?" Cletus' eyes bulged with anger. It looked like they might pop clear out of his head and hit the pavement.

"I don't remember much of it. My mom read it to me and my dad at breakfast."

"What paper's it in?" Warren asked.

"All of them. My mom says they want you to read it. She says they want to make you mad so you will make a mistake." Warren shook his head at Thomas again and he stopped talking. The boy might have already said too much for Cletus to hold his temper.

"So why does your mom know what they're trying to do? She is a lawyer or something?"

"No, but she is smart and figures things out."

"Hum," He walked around to the back of the police car and opened the trunk. There were two-gallon gas cans full of gas. Cops most always had gas in the trunk to help stranded motorists in rural areas. "Warren put this gas in their tank." He turned his attention back to the teenagers. "Because you were so much help, I'm not going to hurt you. Get in the trunk." He pointed to the cruiser. Both kids headed that way. Cletus hit them both hard with the butt of the gun, but not hard enough to kill them. Warren had seen his brother hit people before. If he wanted them dead, they would be.

Cletus closed the trunk, took the keys from the ignition and threw them into a field. They drove off in the Ford.

Warren would worry about the kids. His brother would never give them another thought.

In the next town, Cletus pulled up to a

newspaper vending machine. He got out and paid for a paper, but took two, and tossed one to Warren; drove to the nearest clearing, pulled over and began to read.

Brothers, Cletus and Warren Compton began their life of crime at a young age. Most likely, it became a way of life they learned in childhood.

Their mother Minnie Compton is a criminal herself. She has been in and out of prison for everything from drugs to extortion, prostitution to child endangerment and abandonment, as well as murder.

Division of Family Services records show that Minnie locked the boys in closets for extended periods while she went on with her life.

I am not saying this excuses the Comptons for the laws they have broken and the people they have killed, or the heinous treatment of the children they kidnapped.

I doubt if either of the brothers functions above average. Warren is probably the more intelligent of the two

The part about intelligence sent him into a ballistic fit, causing Cletus to jump out of the car and start to kick the tires.

I would say both brothers are products of child molestation and incest, most likely, at the hands of their mother. It explains why they never hurt the children sexually. It would be like betraying their mother. Cletus especially would not let that happen.

Warren Compton is a little more main stream than his brother. His father raised him for the first six years of his life. It likely gave him a better foundation on which to build.

By all accounts, Warren is the kinder of the two. According to the surviving children, he fed them fruits and vegetables.

"You fed them when I wasn't around?" He buried his head back in the paper and read some more.

It is my opinion that Cletus had a twofold reason for taking the children. The first, money. Compton has collected about two million dollars over the past fifteen or so years. Second, to feed his ego. Cletus constantly needs to feel superior. Each time he took a child, collected a ransom and got by with it, fed his need to show other's his cunning.

The plan began to go wrong when some of the children died of exposure, starvation, and other causes now under investigation by the FBI.

Tomorrow I will discuss how the Compton brother's plan began to fail.

Boo Jordan .M.D., F.A.C.P.

Dr. Jordan is the psychiatrist in charge of debriefing the young victims and helping them readjust to the world. She is the bestselling author of So You Don't Want a Career, Inside the FBI, A Woman's Point of View and Spare the Rod, Spare the Child. Boo Jordan is an FBI profiler.

"Who names their kid Boo?" Cletus screamed.

"Who names their kid, Warren?" He mumbled.

"That stupid father of yours. What a dick. I killed him, you know?"

"No. I didn't know." Cletus was too absorbed to hear the outrage in his brother's voice.

CHAPTER FOURTEEN

The FBI and Tony, along with the Highway Patrol had Ash County well protected. All roads in or out of the area had a trooper, agent or a deputy posted on or hidden around it. They would have liked the National Guard, but to call out the Guard always made the news and they wanted to keep this as quiet as they could.

There were a couple of big ifs in this plan. Did the Comptons read the article? Who knew? Once the piece hit the papers, teasers began to play nationwide on the major networks. They hoped it enraged the fugitives.

The last thing they heard, the men killed a police officer outside a cabin at a fishing lodge on the outskirts of Atlanta. The owner identified Warren Compton as the man who rented the room. No one at the lodge remembered him and the owner said only one man stayed in the room.

They found the officer's cruiser next to the Mississippi State line with two kids in the trunk. The teenagers had contusions, but were otherwise unharmed. The boy said he told Cletus about the newspaper article.

Three days passed with no sightings of the brothers. Tensions were high. Boo and Dean were asked to stay at the camp full time. Boo agreed, Dean refused.

The children who survived the ordeal on Cherokee Ridge were at home asleep in their own beds with a heavy police presence visible at every house.

On October first, north winds began to whistle through the Ozark Mountains.

In the last article, Boo lied and said the camp still housed several children too scared to go home. It alluded to the fact that this had become a safe haven for traumatized children and relieved parents. They were able to come and go at will. They hoped the Comptons would take the bait.

Boo loved to be outside. She liked to walk the trails, ride her horse and collect rocks from the foothills. Since the day they discovered the brothers knew about the scathing articles she wrote, she remained tethered to the main lodge and her office in another building.

After supper, Boo asked Tony to escort her on a short walk to stretch her legs. She felt like a political candidate at election time as agents surrounded her. "Is this necessary?" Her frustration showed.

"Better safe than sorry. Once the first article hit the newspapers, you became a target. It's been three days since any report of a stolen car, a robbery or a sighting. My guess is that they are on their way here."

"Maybe they are smarter than we think they are. Maybe they figured it out and won't come here at all."

Tony looked toward her. "Do you believe that?"

"No. He has to confront the person who called him stupid."

A message arrived at the main gate by way of a teenager in an old black beater pick-up. He said a red haired man flagged him down west of Lindell and paid him a hundred dollars to come to the camp and play a message from the cell phone he held in his hand. They listened.

"This is Cletus Compton. I want to talk to Dr. Boo Jordan. I know she's there. Unless you want something bad to happen in your sleepy town, she'll answer when I call."

The FBI traced the cell phone to George Stanton of Joplin. Authorities were on their way to the Stanton house to check it out.

A few hours later, the Joplin police contacted Tony. George stopped at Radio Shack earlier in the evening to buy a new battery for his phone. He came out of the store and two men jumped him. They took his wallet, and his car, his watch and cell phone.

They found George bound and gagged behind a dumpster near the side of the store. Cold, and terrified but unhurt. George identified them as the two fugitives from the mountain.

The FBI issued a bulletin to all law enforcement agencies on the men and the car. Armed and dangerous, it said. They wanted to catch the criminals, yet without mass chaos if the public found out the killers where in their midst. It might turn out like down south where people shot innocents out of fear it might be one of the brothers.

At six a.m., Boo sat on the edge of her bed trying to decide if coffee or a shower should come first. The phone rang. She smiled. He took the bait. She grabbed the phone and her robe. As she answered the phone, she opened the door. "It's one of the Comptons." She told the guard outside.

"Yes, okay." He bent his chin toward the radio on his shoulder and whispered something into it.

Almost immediately, Juan appeared. He pushed a few buttons on a console on the desk and motioned for her to answer the phone. It rang six times already.

"Did I wake you up?"

The voice she heard was soft with a heavy southern accent. "Yes, yes you did? May I ask who this is?" Boo looked up and smiled at Juan. He gave her two thumbs up.

"Oh, Dr. Jordan, you know who this is. It's me, the dumb product of incest who kidnapped and didn't rape because it would upset his lover mother."

"So good to hear from you. Did my words upset you? It wasn't my intention. I only wanted to explain to people why you do what you do."

"And how can you do that, Dr. Jordan? How can you analyze a man you don't know and have never met?"

His voice rose in anger and Boo smiled. She had him pegged. "I have been in practice many years. I have met other men like you. You aren't that special or different. You had an absent father, a domineering mother, a weak brother and a lousy home life. It's a recipe." Maybe she pushed too hard. She looked at Juan, he mouthed for her to keep talking. "Are you there?"

"Yeah, I'm here. I never raped a child because no one should rape children. You of all people should know that."

"I know that, but since you don't mind killing, why draw the line there? Are you gay, Cletus? Oh, don't get me wrong, being gay is fine. I want to understand." Over the years, she learned the art of how to push a person so far they felt the need to explain themselves, but not so far they hated her.

"I'm going to hang up now. We should talk in person. I'll see you soon."

"Cletus?" He hung up. She looked toward Juan. "Did you get it?"

"Yeah, it's another cell phone. It pinged off a tower in Mt. Vernon. He's getting closer and he's angry. Now if we don't make any mistakes, we should be able to catch him. If we don't get him alive, we can at least put an end to him."

"Here's the thing, Juan. We still know little about Warren. How far will he go to help his brother get here? Let's not count him out. He's a wild card and wild cards have a tendency to muck up everything."

The phone line set up to trace calls rang. Juan answered it. "The phone belongs to a high school student by the name of Heather Gross. She didn't show for school today. The local authorities are out looking for her."

Boo's heart sank. Not another one.

At four o'clock, the police in Mt. Vernon called about Heather. Seems she had skipped school with her boyfriend. They pulled in the driveway the same time they did every day in hopes no one would find out they were truant.

The teenagers had gone to Lindell for the day. They shopped at the Lindell Mall, took a walk at the Nature Center then ate lunch at Red Robin. When they left the mall, the girl couldn't find her phone. They reported it to the woman at the customer service kiosk before they left.

Tony and Ben came in. Boo looked up when Juan spoke.

"What happened?"

Tony walked toward Juan. "It seems like the Compton boys are closer than we thought. They stole a car in Joplin, a 2009 Nissan Sentra, silver, license plate MKL165. When they got to Lindell, they stole a phone from a teenager. Cletus used it to call Boo this afternoon. They are coming after her."

"They might have a different car by now." Ben walked over to the settee and plopped down. He took a drink out of the Coke can he held. "We need to bring Dean here or send more troops his way. Boo's farm is listed in the phone book. They might go there first. If it were me, I'd look around and if no one was home I would break in to see if I could get a read on the occupants."

"We're lucky you are on this side of the law," Tony said.

"I need to call home and warn Dean. It's nearly dark so he should be in the house or the barn. How many men are there?" Boo fretted openly over her husband's safety.

"Only one." Ben picked up his radio and began to speak into it. "Agent Greer, please come to the office."

A minute later, someone tapped on the door. Ben looked out the window before he opened it. "Danny, I know you have been assigned to the Jordan farm a couple of times over the past week. Please take one of Tony's deputies." Ben looked at Tony. "Which one?"

"Deputy Marks. He has only been here since three. The others will change shifts at seven."

"Great." Ben turned back to his agent. "Take Marks and drive over to the Jordan farm. Be alert. The Comptons are close, very close. Make sure Dean is safe. Tell him it would be best for all of us if he would come over here tonight. He can bring his dog. If he has chores to do before he can come, offer to help him. Two of you work, one of you keep a look out. These men are armed and dangerous. If you see anything out of the ordinary, call immediately."

"Roger that." The officer turned on his heel and left.

No one said a word. They each moved over to where Juan rested and picked a place to sit. Tony checked the closed shutters in front of the windows before he joined them.

Boo broke the silence. "I doubt if Dean will be easy to persuade. He doesn't have an enemy in the world or a mean bone in his body. He could never understand the mentality of people like the Comptons."

"I've been doing this for a while now. Thank goodness, there are not many people like the Comptons. But if you listen to the news, you would assume they were a majority." Tony ran his hand thru his thick dark hair. "Most of the criminals I come across are in trouble because of fifteen minutes of bad judgement. I'd say ninety percent of the people I meet would do anything to take back the poor decision they made. That's what makes these men so scary. They, well at least Cletus, don't seem to have any remorse. People like him are born with a character flaw and no one can fix it."

Boo spoke next. "You are more right than you might imagine. There are patterns of antisocial behavior people seem to follow. Cletus has no conscience, assumes he's always the smartest person in the room and needs to prove it repeatedly. It is what makes him so dangerous. He is an enigma."

"In what way?" Ben asked. "He seems textbook to me."

"Because he didn't kill or rape the children. Psychopaths usually have no boundaries. I used to suppose he cared what his brother thought. I don't know what gave me the idea. I was off on that one. I'm convinced he took the kids for the money. He kept the children and chained them because he is sadistic and cruel. He let them go for a reason I have yet to figure out. I suspect the ones who died did so of natural causes, exposure, childhood diseases and dysentery. The kids described the food as a mixture of animal feed grade oats and field corn cooked in chicken stock. Cheap and easy. If Warren had not supplemented their meals, many more would have perished."

"It makes me physically ill to consider it." Juan stood and walked around the perimeter of the room again. "I know they are close, I can feel them."

"I don't suspect they will come at night. Either at dawn with the hopes of catching us off guard or middle of the day. Cletus plans to take his time with the doctor. Our main task now is to make sure he doesn't see the army we have around here." Tony walked to the window.

CHAPTER FIFTEEN

The notorious Compton brothers ditched the Nissan they lifted in Joplin at a mall in Lindell. They picked a truck parked far away from any entrance, in hopes it belonged to an employee who wouldn't notice it missing until the end of the day.

He picked a 2007 Ford F-150 with no pin stripping or fancy wheels to make it stand out.

Warren stole a phone from a man's jacket pocket at a local McDonalds. He looked up the address of Boo Jordan's home. How stupid, to put both husband and wife's name in the listings. He laughed to himself. People made it too easy for him.

.

It took an hour to drive from the main shopping district in Lindell, to Potterville. With the cell phone's GPS, they were able to take a route around the podunk town and get to the farm by way of a secondary road. They left the truck in a field about three hundred yards east of the main driveway. A clump of oaks hid it from sight.

The brothers walked undetected to the back of a big barn. From their vantage point, they surveyed the situation. The Jordans took care of the place. Farm equipment lined a shed to their left. An empty stall alerted them, that someone most likely would come driving up on a tractor before dusk.

As boys, they had lived in houses not as nice as the chicken coop behind them. The main house, a two-story farmhouse with a wraparound porch and window boxes on the ground floor windows sat directly to their right. The upstairs had a balcony outside what they determined to be the master bedroom.

As they took their first step toward the house, they heard a sound. Both men looked at the same time. Moving up the drive at a good clip came a sheriff's cruiser with two officers in it. Cletus had no problem with the prospect of killing both of them. Warren pushed him back behind the barn. "Don't push me. I'm the boss here." He shoved back.

"No one will be boss if we get killed in a shootout with the law," Warren said more and more every day. Cletus had contemplated whether he should kill him or not.

"What's your problem? Do I need to remind you what's at stake here? If we don't get to that doctor, we have no chance of ever being free of all of this."

Warren laughed a little too loud. "If you

believe we are going to get away and ride happily into the sunset, you are crazier than I thought." He snapped his head toward his brother then looked back at the cruiser.

The officers were out of the car by then and Warren noticed they both looked toward the sound. He lowered his voice but finished his thoughts. "We can leave now, try not to call any attention to ourselves and maybe, just maybe, we night make the Mexican or Canadian border. Or we can keep stealing and killing until they put us in the ground."

Cletus drew his arm back and slapped him. The deputies walked toward them and stood only a few feet from the corner of the barn. If they came closer, Warren knew his brother would shoot them. Warren refused to carry a gun. He had his hunting knife strapped to his leg with a new sheath.

As if on cue, a tractor came toward the officers from a field behind the house. As they turned to look, the brothers slipped into the barn and out again by the side door. They were half way back to the woods before anyone checked the noise.

"I should kill you where you stand." Cletus grabbed Warren's shirt.

"Go for it." He put his hands on his hips and stood his ground. "If you are sure I am so dumb and so wrong about the outcome here, what do you suppose is going to happen? Are you going to hunt down that doctor, make her apologize to you and tell you how smart you are? Are you going to kill her too? Do you suppose they will ever let it go that a cop, twenty-two kids, and Boyd are dead at our hand? Do you foresee us ever having a life again? If you fall for that, you are dumber than she said you were!"

He had his gun in his hand and brought it up to his brother's temple. Warren remained in control. "Go ahead. Shoot me. Take me out of this miserable existence I let you rope me into. I can stay in the hell we created or go to the next one. At this point I don't care." For the first time, Warren stood up to his brother. Now the key to survival stemmed on his ability to stand still and not react any more until Cletus calmed down.

"Maybe instead of babying those kids at the camp, you should have read a few books. Maybe you should have read one on free will. You have always had free will. You are free to leave now. I will let you go." Cletus turned and looked back toward the barn. "They're looking for us. I don't want to get caught now. I want to talk to Dr. Jordan. If I do, she can tell our story and set the record straight. I'll suggest she call it: The Compton's, The Story, The Legend. Where are you going?"

"I'm exercising my free will." Warren kept walking, but held his breath, not knowing at what point a bullet would take him down.

Cletus shook his head, put the gun in his belt at the small of his back and crept toward the barn. The three men were inside now. He lay on his belly and crawled under an open window to listen to the conversation inside.

It took him so long to get in positon, the men left before he could learn anything. The tall thin man who lived there walked toward the house and shouted back to the others that he would be ready in about ten minutes. The officers waited near the car.

He could have killed them where they stood but thought better of it. It would be a better move to get the truck and follow them when they left. Warren could stay down so it looked like only one person occupied the cab.

When he got back to the vehicle, there was no trace of Warren. After a quick search of the area, he figured his brother had a hiding place close by and wanted to teach him a lesson. He searched as long as he could, but he had to leave or he would lose the men he wanted to follow. One bag of money and Warren's camping roll were gone

The cops left in the police cruiser and the man followed behind in an old truck with a dog in the front seat beside him. They stopped at the end of the lane. The man in the truck jumped out, locked and chained the front gate and they continued down the road. He waited until they were out of sight to pull onto the road.

Warren, his crazy brother. He convinced himself long ago that he kept his brother around to do the grunt work. What a strange time to worry about him. He shook his head. If Warren wanted to fool around and take the chance of going to jail, let him.

Personally, he wanted to talk to the doctor, convince her to write a story about him that told the truth. Then he would buy a car and go to Canada to live out his life in peace and spend the money he'd horded all these years.

No one would expect him to go to Canada with

winter coming on. To live in Canada was a lifelong dream. After years of study, he knew three or four places to cross the border without detection, lose himself in the population and live happily ever after. Again, the ignorance of people astounded him. Why did people write books about the weaknesses of their borders, how to carry a bomb on an airplane and other equally harmful subjects the public couldn't figure out on their own? Why were people so dumb?

He lost his train of thought and nearly ran into the back of the truck he followed. He slowed down and put his turn signal on so it looked like he wanted to go left at the next road. As luck would have it, the two vehicles turned left there also. Jeez, he needed to pay attention.

For a full ten minutes, he sat with the lights out, and then followed the last road the men had turned on. The next four roads went to the left. The only one with tire tracks went to a camp.

CAMP MOCCASIN, BOY SCOUTS OF AMERICA. MAIN ENTRANCE. SERVICE VEHICLES USE NEXT DRIVE.

Two armed guards lounged near the front gate. Cletus drove on by; the guards were talking and didn't pay any attention. The camp had been around for decades. It backed up to Cherokee Ridge on the west.

Cletus had total recall. He loved to say, "I have forgotten more than most people will ever know."

One more time he drove back to the Jordan farm and down all the roads near it.

No sign of Warren.

"Stupid kid." He banged his fist on the steering wheel. "I hope he doesn't get me caught."

Twenty minutes later, he pulled up in front of the Lindell Public Library. After taking the time to cover his hair with a ball cap and tuck his shirt in, he went inside. The rest of the evening, he read about the Boy Scout camp.

It sat on 557 acres. An online brochure showed all the buildings and trails. No way, did they have the entire place guarded.

At a farm and home store on the west side of the city he bought dark clothes, a dark hat and coat. Then picked out hiking boots, a sleeping bag, backpack and hunting knife. It might take hours to reach Dr. Jordan. It might take days. Be prepared, The Boy Scout motto, he congratulated himself for his cleverness.

Night had settled in and with it a chilly north wind. Missouri used daylight savings time and he hated it. It got dark so early. At an all-, you- can-eat steak house, he gorged himself.

The ride back to Ash County took almost forty-five minutes. There were no streetlights on the country roads to alert anyone to his presence. On a dark lonely road, behind a stand of trees, he parked the truck. With a branch from a sticky cedar tree, he covered any tracks, made a bed in the back of the truck and climbed in.

He slept until the next morning when a sunbeam hit him in the face and woke him. Once he folded the gear so it was easy to carry, he drove closer to the camp. About five miles south of it, he hid the truck again, secured the sleeping bag to his backpack, and began to hike toward the highest point on the map.

Cletus remained lean. He loved to hike on Cherokee Ridge; he could walk for miles and never see another human.

Two and a half hours into his uphill trek and he wasn't winded. The path meandered through the woods and had arrows now and then to mark the way. Not one person crossed his path. The only sounds he heard were birds and the rustle of small animals and lizards as they moved away. He felt safe and secure, even in the spots where the path curved out around a cliff putting him on parts of the path where he had no cover at all.

At a point where the trees and brush didn't obscure the view, he looked below at the camp compound. A muffled sound drifted his way. He fell to the ground and began to crawl on his belly toward it. Two men in uniform sat in a clearing. They had a clear view of the camp. One smoked a cigarette; the other drank a Coke.

They had the place under guard.

Over years and many hours of being locked up in dark closets, came patience. He scooted toward the tallest bushes in the area and prepared to wait. An hour later, one of the men stood and walked toward the woods away from him. Before the other man could react, Cletus grabbed him from behind and quietly slit his throat and dragged him to the brush as he bled to death.

With the knife back in the leather cover, he crawled silently up to the point where the second officer stepped into the woods and moved back out of sight. As the highway patrol officer came out of the woods, Cletus tripped him, jumped on top of him, pinned him down and put his hand over the man's mouth. "Do you know who I am?" He smiled his yellow toothed smile.

The trapped man signaled with his eyes, and a little nod, that he did.

"Your friend is dead." With those words, he pulled the knife out and stuck it right into the man's heart. He sat on his chest until the life went out of the officer's eyes, then got on his hands and knees and pushed on the officer's chest to watch the last of the blood drain out.

It took another hour to pull the second man into the woods, cover the bodies and clean up the blood. Then he laid down on the summit and looked down on the camp below. "This will be easy,"

The rest of the day, he studied, counted people, buildings, steps and planned how to breach the camp. He would go down as soon as the sunset, about five or six hours. Less than twenty feet from the bodies, he put his sleeping bag behind his head and took a nap.

He remained covered with blood. Before he settled in, he took some dirt and rubbed it on his hands and arms to make them less sticky. He wiped the knife on the ground, rolled over and went to sleep. He never gave the two cops another thought.

CHAPTER SIXTEEN

Warren walked south and ducked out of sight when the police drove by. His brother followed in the stolen truck. He stepped further into the woods and watched undetected.

The smug look on Cletus' face stirred the hate from earlier in the day when he walked away.

At times, he wanted to run far and fast, but never before did he sink to hate like today.

When it felt safe again, he went back to the road and walked until the sound of a car scared him. He dove into the deep underbrush and stayed five minutes after it went by. He learned from robbing people that they saw only what they expected to see. If they walked past an alley night after night and no one jumped out, soon they never bothered to look.

If someone jogged the same path day after day, and never saw a dog, a dog could come out and bite them before they saw it. Same way with muggers and robbers. People are creatures of habit and constantly distracted. Everyone has an exercise tracker on her arm or a phone in his hand. It makes it so easy for any would be criminal to attack his victim.

Never again did he intend to participate in his older brother's murderous plans. Memories of life before Mama and Cletus faded every year, but the flashback of his father's touch and smile kept him going these days.

Cletus killed him.

It could be true or it could be another method of control. He couldn't bear to find out which.

Tears streamed from his eyes. He willed himself to get up and stop his look back to the past. Nothing could change it. Today couldn't be lost in a longing for yesterday.

Cletus had a plan to go to Canada because no one would expect it.

He would go to Mexico. With half the money, he could go anywhere and do anything. A crappy plan beat no plan at all.

About a mile down the road a mailbox sat by the edge of the road. It had Homer Doling hand painted in faded red. He walked up the drive, careful to hug the edge of the sparse gravel in case someone turned in.

A house sat at the end of the drive. It used to be white, now it cried for paint. The windows wore years of grime and cement blocks served as steps. He had a flashback to the cabin on Cherokee Ridge.

"Good." Warren breathed. "The place is

abandoned." He would stay there until he had a real plan.

Maybe they would catch Cletus, and then he could go to Canada and live in the wilderness. He preferred it to Mexico; however, Mexico alone beat Canada with Cletus.

He walked up the stairs and across the porch, avoiding the places he could fall through; he cupped his hands and looked in the windows. To his surprise, a dim light shined through the dirt. Warren walked to the door and knocked. It had no latch and creaked open. In a chair, next to a fireplace with no fire, sat an old man. He appeared dead.

"Whose there? Donald, it that you?" The old man's voice sounded weak.

Warren walked closer to the chair and knelt down. "Is this your house, old man?"

"Donald. I didn't reckon you would ever get here. The fire is out." When the man looked up Warren saw a white film covered the center of each eye.

"Sorry it took me so long. Are you hungry?" This might be a blessing for the young Compton.

"Cold and hungry. The fire has been out for a while. Maybe yesterday or the day before."

"When do I usually come see you?" A thought flashed though his mind that if his brother had found the old man, he would have killed him by now.

"Before you went off to war, you came all the time. Two soldiers came last week and said you were dead. I knew they were wrong. I knew you wouldn't leave me."

"No, Grandpa, I would never leave you." The boy must have served in Iraq. If he died there, he couldn't be a son, had to be a grandson.

"Who made the last fire?"

"The men who came about you. They built a fire and brought in firewood. Come closer so I can see you."

He took a deep breath and scooted closer. The man put his hand on his visitor's unshaved face and smiled. "There is a God," Grandpa said.

It had to be Homer Doling. Warren figured he had lived a hard eighty years or an easy ninety plus.

Warren spent the rest of the day building a fire, stacking firewood in the house, fixing the old man some soup, and then he cleaned the kitchen and swept the filthy floors. On the back porch there sat an old wringer washer. It proved a challenge. However, he managed to launder all the bedding and clothes he found and hung them across a make shift line off the back porch.

It got too dark for him to wander around outside. He smiled. This was a foreign experience and he loved it.

His life became lies, stealing, beatings, kidnappings and all the money anyone could ever want. Of course, Cletus would never let him spend much of it for fear someone would become interested in why they could buy whatever they wanted. He had to live in a shack on the Ridge, with ratty furniture and old cars and trucks and clothes.

For the first time in his adult life, he felt proud. He took time to smile down at Grandpa then walked through the house. A once prime and proper house, it suffered from lack of care and paint. He picked up the picture on the mantel, opened the medicine cabinet in the bathroom and went through all the drawers and cabinets.

Homer wasn't a poor man; he had accumulated some pretty items. Warren respected his property and left it alone.

"Grampa?" He gently shook the man. "Let's get you out of that chair. You've been there for hours. Can't be good for you."

Homer got up with the younger man's help. Warren towered over the old man whose back curved downward so far, he looked at his own feet as he walked "Hand me my cane. I can still get around."

Warren put him in the shower and stayed in the bathroom while the man got weeks of grim off his body. He helped him shave, made him a sandwich for dinner and put him in bed. Again, he smiled. Is this what made him happy, small, tedious, backbreaking chores? He sat on the porch for hours and listened to the sounds of a country night.

Warren relaxed. Oh, to live happily ever after right there, with Homer Doling, would be a version of heaven.

CHAPTER SEVENTEEN

After years of marriage, Boo could easily read Dean's moods. A man who went outside at dawn, came in for lunch and then went back out until dusk, sat locked in a room for three days. Jack, his yellow lab, dogged his every step and looked as bored as his master.

If Dean wanted to walk the dog, it looked like a platoon on maneuvers, two guards in front, two guards at his sides and two behind him.

"My idea is that we take this posse to the farm. I need to feed hay and tend to my orchards. Not to mention I'm bored stiff. I feel like a child in time out. Can't you do something? Right now, I would welcome a run in with our two fugitives. At least we would be doing something," Dean threw down the Outdoor Home magazine he had in his hand and walked over to a window to peer out.

His wife got up from her desk chair in the room where she talked to the kids. She came to where he stood. From behind, she put her arms around his waist and leaned against his back. "I feel the same way. They said our fugitives were in Lindell, I thought they would be here by now. Maybe they are smarter than I thought."

The door opened with such force it banged against the wall. Agent Ben Goodman had to raise his arm to protect himself from the backswing. Right behind him were Agent Gomez and Sheriff Massey. Boo looked from one man to another. They were all ghostly gray.

"What happened, Sheriff?" Dean asked before his wife had a chance.

"The patrol cars of the men on guard at the summit last night are still in the parking lot. The younger officer's mother called, worried because he didn't make it home last night. The other man's wife is at the front gate with a lunch for him. I have men headed up there see what happened." Tony walked closer to Boo as he talked. "I have a bad feeling about this. We want to go ourselves, but it might be a scheme to get you alone, Boo "

"I'm here." Dean answered.

Ben put his hand on Dean's shoulder. "I don't want to hurt your feelings, sir, but have you ever killed a man?"

"No, but to protect my wife, I could."

"Again, no insult intended, but these men would kill you while you thought about what to do next." Ben turned his attention to Boo. "Are you armed?"

"I have a 9 millimeter in the drawer. But I would be dead before I could get too it," she answered.

"I will get you both a service weapon." Tony headed for the door then stopped. "I'll put a guard at both doors and make sure the windows are locked. I notice the dog didn't bark when we barged in."

"No, he would if we were home. He's out of his element." Dean glanced at Boo and she smiled at him. "If he barked at everything out of the ordinary here, he would never shut up."

Ten minutes later, Tony came back with two tactical vests, two Glock 22's and a 12-gauge shotgun. He helped the Jordan's arm themselves and left without as much as a word.

Before he could close the door, the radio on his shoulder crackled. "We found two bodies. One with his throat cut and the other stabbed in the chest." Tony staggered to a chair, sat down and rested his chin in his hands.

Boo walked to him. "I'm so sorry Tony. It just gets worse and worse. It won't end until they are both dead. It is the only way to stop them."

Ben and Juan walked through the doorway toward Tony. "Sorry about your man. Captain Harris is at the gate with his man's wife. I'm sure you want to notify your Sergeant's mother," Juan said.

"This place is going to be a madhouse in an hour or so. The medical examiner and a CSI team are on the way," Ben added.

Tony stood. "Is Macy Adam's still at the gate?"

Boo watched the men. "Would you men like to talk about what happened before you go any further?"

"We'll talk when this is over. Right now, we need to keep moving." Ben headed toward the door. The other two followed.

Boo approached her husband and wiggled into his arms. "I haven't missed this in the last fifteen years. Until I found the girl by the side of the road, I had myself convinced that we lived far enough away from the life I once had to have it affect me again. I guess I was wrong."

"This'll all be over soon." Dean kissed the top of her head. "None of us will ever be the same though. Events like this touch so many people. In this case, people all over the country. So many families torn and twisted. It's a true national tragedy. Makes me long for the greenhouse and the sweet smell of orchids."

They stood together, each lost in thought, neither made an attempt to move.

CHAPTER EIGHTEEN

Before daylight Cletus Compton sneaked down the hill and stood in the shadows under the north window to watch and listen to the people inside. The conversation they'd had made him want to laugh. *What a bunch of pansies!*

Killing the two cops last night might have been a mistake. Not because the murders weighed on his conscience, but because the meeting with Dr. Jorden would have to wait another day. That meant an additional cold night in a sleeping bag.

As he looked in he saw that Boo Jordan stood tall, straight and was bean pole skinny. Not at all attractive. Women needed a little meat on their bones like... well... Mama.

The sheriff handed the Jordans hand guns, fitted them with bulletproof vests and propped a shotgun next to the desk. Jeez, weapons were no deterrent.

This visit had nothing to do with killing. Cletus wanted the good doctor to retract her articles and write the truth. Explain about the kidnappings, robberies, murders, but most of all about his sexuality and special relationship with Mama.

Once Boo told the truth, the reign of terror would be over. His new life wouldn't include violence. Fishing, hunting, and reading topped the list of new endeavors at the new home he planned to make Canada. Maybe the authorities would catch him, but either way, no longer would the prospect of getting caught rule his life. He would never run again. No matter what.

If Warren hadn't left, it would have been easier to get away. At this point, it made no difference. The only goal here included the doctor and the truth according to Cletus Compton.

The conversation inside paused. Everyone left except the doctor and her husband and they all they were doing was hugging. How boring.

With boredom came hunger. There were spells when food dominated his day and week's food was the furthest thing from his mind. The cafeteria had a carved sign over the door, mess hall. The building stood forty yards from the window. No one looked his direction as he started toward it. Then he heard the sheriff speak to the men in a central circle.

"Finally, we have some pertinent information about how we'll protect the Jordans. The operation will move to the doctor's farm where it will be easier to capture the Comptons."

To keep a deer you are hunting from seeing you

approach, a hunter moves one-step at a time, stops, waits then does it again. Eventually the deer can no longer escape. He was using the hunter's tactics and that is how he got to the cafeteria unnoticed. People were so stupid. He reached the back door of the dining hall unnoticed. No one could see him now.

The windows shed the only light. He cupped his hands and looked inside, then tried the door and it creaked open. The items in the huge pantry at the back of the room were exposed. A bonanza of food donned every shelf. Canned beef stew, soup, crackers, snack cakes, peanut butter, rice, and a host of other items made up a beggar's dream. After making a hobo sack out of a dishtowel, he filled it with his favorites. On the way out door, he took two sodas and stuck them in the pockets of his jeans.

The doors, of the building the doctor and her husband were in, were now guarded. From the other end of the porch, the parking lot was visible. There were two cars left. He grinned.

They were looking for two men. They weren't looking in the right place. Maybe if he shouted and waved his arms the law could find him. *Doubtful.* That ungrateful brother of his might already be in Mexico or Canada. "If I see him, I will kill him myself." Did he say that aloud?

With the pack slung over his shoulder, his gun stowed in the waistband of his pants near the zipper, and enough food for a week, it was time to go. Rather than climb again, he chose a well-marked trail near the camp's service road

After an hour of hiking, he stopped then used his finger to spread peanut butter on a dozen crackers to eat along the way. By midafternoon, he reached the road that lead to freedom. The blacktop went up hill or downhill. Most people would pick the easiest route so he went the opposite way. For them to catch him, he would have either to turn himself in or yell, yoohoo, here I am. Cops were stupid people

Right before dark, he found the perfect camping spot, about a hundred yards off the road. He could see in every direction and hear the road noises. It took an hour to set up camp. With deep woods behind him and to the left, a dozen cedar trees in front of him and around to the right, completely hidden from the road that he could almost reach out and touch.

Farmers called these cedar glades natural barns. The trees grew close together and gave shelter from wind, rain, animals and in this case people. Even without a fire, the brush would deter animals. If a creature did make it through, the undergrowth made it impossible for it to attack. Cletus popped the tab on one of the sodas and leaned back to admire this handiwork.

Sleep came almost immediately. When he woke, hours later, a harvest moon lit the entire sky. "Damn you Warren, why did you leave?" he asked the moon, but the moon didn't answer.

No one would need a flashlight to walk around on this night. The full moon and the light it projected were a plus. However, the police were too worried about their fallen men and the doctor's safety to go out traipsing about the countryside to look for killers. He knew he was safe her for at least another day.

The food he'd stolen only lasted one day. He rubbed his belly and figured skinny as he was he probably looked like a snake that swallowed an egg.

The forty-five now rested under the sleeping bag. With a little practice, he could pull it out and shoot in one fluid motion. Sleep was the goal for tonight. Tomorrow the goal would be to confront the doctor.

CHAPTER NINETEEN

On the drive out to Deputy Darren Michael's place, Tony went over his prepared speech.

The long driveway curved up to a modest home on about three acres on the edge of town. Last year, after the death of his father, Darren moved in with his mom. Tony glanced around. Darren kept the place the neat and clean.

Ellen Michael walked out the front door before the SUV had a chance to stop.

"Where is he?" Her voice squeaked higher than usual.

Tony shook his head. "I have bad news, Mrs. Michael."

"Was it those awful Compton brothers?" She fell against the sheriff.

"An educated guess? I would say yes, but we don't know for sure. Let's go in, out of the wind."

Tony put his hand on her waist to try to move her toward the door.

When Darren's mother failed to move, he increased the pressure. This would never get easier. Tony could and would say all the right words, but truth be told, how one person could kill another remained a mystery to him.

Every night on the news, someone killed someone. It took a special kind of monster to take another's life force, to see the light forever fade from another's eyes.

"Tony, tell me what happened."

"Darren and a state trooper had guard duty at the summit. The terrain makes it impossible to move around up there after dark."

"How did my boy die?"

Tony turned toward her in surprise. "Does it matter?"

"Yes."

"Stabbed." Tony chocked the word out. "He didn't suffer, death was instant. Let me call someone for you. This is no time to be alone."

"Darren's sister and brother will be here soon. They are coming for a family dinner." She looked at a clock on the wall. "They will be here any minute. Until then, Sheriff, I will be fine. I could actually use a couple of minutes alone before they arrive."

Tony stood. "I'll get out of your way then."

"Darren thought the world of you."

Tears welled in the sheriff's eyes. To try to stop them was fruitless. Once in the car, Tony made a promise. "I intend to put an end to the Compton brothers."

On the way back, Tony decided to stop at the farms along the way. Maybe someone saw someone or something out of the ordinary. What could it hurt? The camp was dark with mourning. To see someone else and talk about something else would be a needed mental distraction.

Most of the farmers were in the fields doing chores or in their barns. They waved; some jumped down and walked to the fence to speak with him. The men and women in their barns and workshops were equally friendly. They hoped for news.

Tony turned the cruiser into the Homer Doling's driveway. It looked different; mowed, weeds pulled, porch swept and the windows cleaned. Except for the sound of Homer's TV, the place remained ghostly quiet.

Tony reached to knock on the door. The screen door hung straight for the first time in years.

"Who's there?" The voice belonged to the old man.

"It's me, Sheriff Massey, can I come in?" Tony had the door half open.

"Sure, Tony, I could use the company. What brings you out here today?"

Again, the sheriff looked around. The room shined. A fire roared in the fireplace, a tray of food sat on the arm of the old lounge chair. An entire corner of the room held neatly stacked firewood, small enough for Mr. Doling to handle. Tony couldn't remember if he ever saw the old man clean shaven.

"My, Homer. This place sure looks nice. Who's doing all this for you?" Tony tried to keep all emotion out of his voice. "Is someone living with you?" Due to the recent events, the regular rounds the sheriff made to check on Ash County's citizens had ceased. These older defenseless people in the country would be in sad shape if the Comptons dropped by.

"Oh, it's the Timber Ridge folks, been coming by regularly for a few weeks now. I hope they keep it up. I could get used to this."

"Is Earl Parkinson still in charge over there?"

"Yes, that's the guy. Nice group. Been here every week. How are things in town?" Homer sat the tray on the floor next to him.

"Do you still get the paper, Homer?"

"No sheriff, I can't see to read much anymore. I listen to the radio."

"So you know about the two brothers who had a place on Cherokee Ridge, went on a killing spree and all of that."

Homer looked happy and at ease. "Yes, I know about it. Haven't seen a soul, other than those church people, I don't get much company."

"Well, lock your doors and take care of yourself Homer. We know those boys are close by. They kill just to be killing. Keep that shotgun close."

"I do. It's right here." He bent down and touched the barrel. The tray of food rested half next to it."

"Here, let me take that tray to the kitchen for you." Tony noticed the small things, the floors swept, sink, and the pantry neat and tidy. "I wish the Timber Ridge folks would drop by my house. Is there anything I can do for you before I go?"

"No, those folks were here yesterday and the wood is chopped small enough I can handle it myself. Let me know when the neighborhood is safe again."

Tony smiled, and walked back to the car. He would have to thank Earl next time they met. What a great group of people to take care of the old folks in their community.

Tony got back to the camp a little before noon. The place bustled with activity. "What's up?" No one bothered to radio the sheriff.

"Someone broke in the mess hall and helped themselves to some food. They came in through the back. We went out in groups of four to look around, found a soda can and two wrappers down the narrow path to the main road. Someone either is here or has been here."

"Who's with Dr. Jordan and her husband?"

"Agent Goodman and some of his men. I think it's the Comptons."

Tony turned red. "Thanks," he said and headed to the office.

Tension loomed in the room. Boo paced. Dean flipped through a gardening magazine, Ben and his men guarded the windows and door. "Good to have you back," Ben said. "We have had a development."

"I heard." Tony stood legs apart and hands on his hips. "Let's end this once and for all." There's no way they are coming here with all of these guards and agents. It's time we make a show of packing up and moving the Jordan's home. If we send men ahead to hunker down in the barn and the greenhouses, we can keep the focus on the move and us. The logistics are in our favor at the farm."

"I agree," Boo said.

"Let's tear this place down. We'll give the men time to get in position and then we disband. I'll go back to the office. We'll send the highway patrol on their way and you guys go back into town." With his last comment, Tony pointed to Juan and Ben.

"How can we keep Boo from being the next target, or keep Dean safe around the farm? If we want to make sure they assume we gave up on them, they'll need a believable reason. You don't just stop looking for the two men at the top of the most wanted list. They know that."

"First we put out a statement about our men and their murders. We say we know who did it and it wasn't the Compton brothers. The man also broke into the camp and stole food."

"I don't know, Tony. Two of our men are dead already. I consider the men in great danger if they are in the barn or the greenhouses. You, Juan, and I need do this, nobody else. I'll take the first shift." Ben stood and took a step toward Boo. "The key is to stay out of sight and try to make it look like you're back to normal. However, they won't believe we all gave up. They aren't stupid. We need a story. How about, they were spotted in Mobile, a high-speed chase ensued and their car exploded on impact when it hit a bridge. We'll say the bodies were burned beyond recognition, but that we have positive identification. What do you think?"

"It could work, but I agree, there is no way to

protect Dean if he's away from the house feeding or something." Boo glanced at her husband.

"We have him sprain his ankle right here in front of the building. It would give us a reason to keep him inside so we can protect him." Tony knew Dean would have an objection. He raised his hand to stop him. "Wait, Dean, look at it this way. We can draw them to the farm in a day or two or we can sit here for what might be weeks, and wait."

Dean shook his head. "Fine, I'll do it. Let's get this over with."

Tony smiled. "It will take a little while to set it up. We need surveillance, someone to drop us off so there are no cars and about twenty other items on my list. If everyone agrees, we'll get the ball rolling."

Ben scratched his head. "I'm in agreement except for one thing. We three should go in together. Once we get set up, it will be nearly impossible to change from one of us to another."

"He's right," Juan chimed in for the first time.

CHAPTER TWENTY

Warren Compton listened to every word the sheriff and Homer Doling said to one another. He stood close to the back wall in the pantry and prayed the sheriff would not come any further, but he did.

Warren's heart beat hard when the officer came into the kitchen. The man glanced in the cupboard and Warren had the hunting knife poised and ready to use. However when the sheriff turned and walked out of the room, he relaxed his arm and dropped the hand holding the knife, to his side. His heart began to slow and tension flowed out of his body.

Unhappiness is not something a person wants to dwell on, but Warren had no happy memories as an adult. The life he'd lived with the old man for the past week brought unknown joy, but now it was time to go.

Sheriff Massey would be back in a day or a

week, maybe as long as a month. Once he found out the Timber Ridge people had nothing to do with the firewood, the clean windows, the food or anything else, Warren would get caught or worse, Homer might get in trouble for lying.

Following his brother's escapades on Homer's radio was the only way he knew what was going on. It blasted country music, news and weather twenty-four hours a day.

A bulletin came on the radio that said someone at the camp killed two law officers. They warned people to lock their doors and keep their children close. They said the suspect was in custody and the man had nothing to do with the Comptons.

Poor guy got blamed for something Cletus probably did. On the other hand, maybe they thought *he* did it. Every description of him mentioned the foot long knife strapped to his left leg by a bandana. This bulletin said the men died from knife wounds. Even more reason to leave.

Warren slid down the wall and sat on the floor with his legs straight out in front of him, to reorganize his thoughts. For the first time, he loved someone, and hated to leave Homer, but if Cletus happened to stumble onto the place, the old man would be dead.

Tears streamed down his face. Never before had he wept for another human, not even himself. He had learned that crying made it worse when his brother did things to him like terrorizing him with alligators and snakes from the bayou. So he kept his feelings hidden.

What a fool to allow dreams that he could have

a life here after what he did.

Why did he blindly follow Cletus and kill Boyd? He couldn't believe he stood by and watched child after child be brought to the mountain, chained and half-starved and did little or nothing about it. When his brother shot the kid in the diner, he watched and said nothing. He helped pick out the cars they stole and the people they robbed.

He wiped his wet cheeks with the sleeve of his shirt. He knew what was going to happen. When Cletus sat in a cell on death row, he would be in the one next to him.

Thirty minutes later, with his emotions under control, he went to say goodbye to Homer. Self-preservation took hold and old habits surfaced. Warren sat under a window with his back to the wall and eyes on the driveway. "I heard what you told the sheriff." He ran the back of his hand over his eyes to wipe away the rest of the tears.

"Yes, son, I reckon he was satisfied. I don't see him coming back anytime soon." Homer grinned.

His voice remained quiet and calm. "Why didn't you just tell him your grandson came home?"

"Because we buried him five years ago and Sheriff Massey attended the funeral."

He leaned forward not believing what he'd just heard. "So… you've known all along who I am?"

Homer chuckled. "Yes, they give your description over and over on the radio. Son, when you get as old as I am you learn a few things; my gift is to judge the character of men. I knew you would never hurt me."

"And you think I am a good man, Homer?"

"I do."

"Well, I'm not. I am so bad, I'm afraid to die. I'm a coward who foresees an eternity in Hell so I keep going as long as possible."

"Well, Warren, there are men who have tried to be good all of their lives and are still afraid to die for the same reason." The old man slowly bowed his head.

Warren thought he fell asleep, until he saw the tears. It broke his heart.

"You're going to leave now, aren't you?"

"I'll have to. When the sheriff realizes the church people aren't doing the chores around here, he will be back with more men to make sure you are safe." He stood, moved next to Homer's chair and knelt. Then he did something out of character, he put his head in the man's lap. Homer stroked Warren's hair. Did the man really care?

"I'm sorry I couldn't think of what to say to him. All anyone has to do is see your face and they'll know who you are. I recognized you right away and I don't get out much. You're quite distinctive. Where will you go?"

"I'll go over to the camp and find Cletus. If I can, I am going to try persuading him to leave. There's been enough killing." He backed away from the old man and prepared to leave. No tears this time. "There's still some beef stew in the refrigerator. Do you need anything before I go?"

"No, but I have an idea. Why don't you stay here and when the sheriff comes back you can peacefully turn yourself in?" Now the old man shed tears openly.

"It won't end that way, Homer, and you know it." In silence, he packed the meager possessions he came with. Most of his gear he hid in a cave about a mile down the lane.

Warren lingered in the doorway, quiet and still. He took in every sight, sound and smell. "I'll miss you, old man."

"I'll miss you too, son. God bless you."

"Oh, Homer. It's too late for that. God turns the other way when I try to talk to him. If he didn't, he would have helped me stop this evil long ago."

CHAPTER TWENTY ONE

The plan put in place by the FBI agents and Tony Massey might not work. It had been a long time since Boo profiled for the FBI, and she was concerned but a criminal mind remained the same.

Sociopaths and psychopaths had patterns. Both of these antisocial behaviors shared a trait, lack of restraint. For this to be a success, they had better move fast. The assumption that the Comptons no longer had transportation bothered her. Of course, they did, and could easily beat the officers to the farm if they got wind of the plan.

The only people left at the camp, besides herself, were the two guards outside the doors. They were to protect her while the rest of the team set up the farm for the operation. They set up communications and secured the outbuildings while watching for the brothers.

Deep breathing usually calmed her, but not today. The criminals killed two guards before, so why would the two here pose no roadblock? She had the heebie-jeebies. Experience warned her something would happen soon.

Boo started to inform the guards of her concerns, but she saw Cletus standing inside the guarded backdoor. "I didn't hear you come in." She sat back in her chair and tried to calm her nerves.

"Now what kind of criminal would I be if you could hear me coming?"
He grinned a yellow-toothed grin that turned her stomach. She reached down and slid the desk drawer open to retrieve the gun. Cletus spoke soft, but firm.

"Put both hands on the desk and scoot away from it." Boo remained in her chair. "Boo, you don't want to make me angry. I didn't come here to hurt you, but I will if I need to."

She moved to the side of the desk, but stayed in the chair as she scooted out of the way. She wouldn't balk him at this point.

He walked over, opened the drawer and took out the weapon. He glanced at it and grinned, then looked at this own gun. In a great show of movement, Cletus put her gun in his shooting hand and tucked the other one in the waistband of his jeans. "Boo, is an unusual name. What's your real name?"

"That *is* my name. So you came all this way to find out if Boo is my real name?" Cletus flushed and it alerted her to his frustration. Everyone had a *'tell'*. It was a small thing a person did before they explode, laugh or lie and this was his. She wanted a balance, keep him angry and off guard but not so much he would kill her. If he talked long enough one of the crew would come back. Someone checked on her every half an hour or so.

"Do you know why I'm here?"

The color in his face returned to normal. As normal as a filthy man who'd spent days in the woods without so much as cleaning his hands, or combing his short, curly hair could be.

"I have a pretty good idea. You would like to talk to me about the articles I wrote for the newspapers." To reinforce the fact she didn't scare easily, she folded her arms and leaned on one arm of the chair.

"I want you to let me tell you what I'm like. I want you to take what you learn about the real me and write some more stories. Set the record straight, so to speak. I have reasons for everything I've done."

"Why did you take those kids?"

"For the money."

"Tell me why the children were kept captive. The parents paid the ransom you tortured the kids anyway." He seemed indignant and it angered her.

"I didn't torture them. I gave them a place to sleep, food and eventually the money to get back home."

Boo decided to change the subject. "Where is your brother?"

"He's outside, keeping an eye on the guards."

A lie, the red face again. This would be fun if she could ignore the blood from the two police officers now dried on his jeans; or the bloody hand prints on the once white tee shirt and the smell of sweat, blood, dirt and body odor consuming the air in the room. "How long has it been since you cleaned up?"

"You are about to hurt my feelings. Do you think I need a shower?"

Boo, as a trained FBI agent could take care of herself. People forgot that. They saw her as a doctor, and therefore, no threat. When she worked for the bureau, she used her brain more than her weapon. The only man she ever killed she killed on her last day of work nearly fifteen years ago. The look on the dying man's face, when the light went out of his eyes, lingered all these years.

This man, she could kill without remorse, and her attitude put her in danger. The doctor closed her eyes and took a deep breath. She had to say in control.

When she opened her eyes, he had taken another step closer. Every one of her senses peaked to high alert. At the slightest distraction, Boo would make her move. Perhaps he would glance away. She needed only a moment to jump him and get control of the gun. She sized him up and knew she could take him down. She could overpower someone twice her size without breaking a sweat.

The ruckus would alert the guards outside and it would all be over. For the first time in her life hate for someone overtook her need to talk to him, to see what made him tick. With his man, his eyes told it all. They were green, unresponsive and scary. She followed his line of vision and determined he looked through her, not at her. His pupils were huge, and transfixed.

A noise came from the front of the cabin. Cletus looked toward it. Boo made her move. She pushed herself out of the chair with both hands, leapt over the corner of the desk and landed on his chest. The gun fell from his hand and slid across the floor toward the door.

The door opened and she looked up. She recognized Warren when he stepped in. He had a bloody knife in one hand and a Gideon Bible in the other.

He stopped and screamed, "Move away from her!" His brother, who had gained control of the situation and had a chokehold on Boo.

Temporarily disoriented, Cletus grinned from ear to ear when he realized Warren had come to help him. He squeezed harder on Boo's neck until she went limp and fell out of his grip. "I'm glad to see you, brother. I knew you'd come back." The doctor regained some air but lay quiet until she had enough strength to move out of the way and out of his reach. He let her move.

He focused all of his attention on Warren. "Where have you been?"

"Away from you."

Cletus looked at Warren when he heard the hate and anger in his voice. He put his arms out and faked wanting a hug. "Come here, brother."

Warren ran toward him, the hunting knife poised between them like an extension. Was his brother going to kill him? "Stop! Don't make me shoot you, Warren." He awkwardly reached for the gun in the waistband.

Warren picked up speed. Cletus had no chance to move, his brother fell into him full force. Pain shot through him somewhere between his heart and his upper belly. Was this the end?

Boo heard the blood gurgle out of the hole in Cletus' gut. The floor turned crimson so fast she stood and moved away. She scrambled toward the door but stopped when she heard Cletus say in a dying gasp.

"How could you?"

She watched Warren fall to his knees. He knelt over his dying brother with no emotion on his face.

"See you in Hell, Cletus. We can talk then."

Boo watched in horror when Warren raised the knife as high as he could, bent his arms and shoved the blade toward his own chest then jammed it in. He fell, face forward on the floor beside his brother. The Comptons lay side by side; their blood swirled together in the center of the room.

When she regained her composure, she ran to the door, opened it and stepped out. The guard lay alive, but was bound and gagged near a tree in the courtyard. She went back inside, stepped around the two dead men, grabbed the letter opener and went to cut him loose.

Together they hurried to the back door where the other officer lay unconscious and bleeding. While the guard helped the man, Boo went inside and called 911. She heard the voice on the other end.

"What is the nature of your emergency?"

"Please send an ambulance to Camp Moccasin. Three people down. One officer injured, two suspects dead." She hung up then walked out the front door to get away from the smell of blood.

CHAPTER TWENTY TWO

During the next two weeks, Boo told her story several times, once to the FBI, then again at the Coroner's inquest and of course to Dean.

The kidnapped victims would have an easier time adjusting to life again. The bad men were dead.

Two duffle bags of money lay in an evidence locker in Tulsa. All involved wanted the money divided among the surviving children. Minnie Compton filed a suit in Federal Court as the only living relative of the brothers. It laid out how she deserved the money because her sons earned it. Now, her boys were gone she had no support.

In a hollow tree near the makeshift camp Cletus fashioned in the woods, authorities found two notebooks. In small neat printing were the names and ages of the kidnapped children, dated back seventeen years. The other book contained the dates of release and the amount of each ransom. If a child died for any reason, the last column contained a big red D.

Boo couldn't go back to writing fluffy self-help books. She roamed around the farm, watched the sunrise and set each day and spent time with Dean while he tended his orchids. For now, she wanted to be in nature, and rest in quiet, and count her blessings.

Tony dropped by now and then.

About the time she had it all sorted out in her head, the phone rang. "Hello?"

"Hi Boo, It's me Juan Gomez."

"What can I help you with, Juan?"

"We have a case down here. A mass murder at a Girl Scout camp on the edge of town. Twelve young girls slaughtered. It has been two years and we have yet to find a witness or a suspect. We would like you to come down and look at everything we have. Maybe you could figure out a profile or at least point us in another direction.

"I'd have to ask Dean."

"Ask me what?" Dean said as he came in the room.

ABOUT THE AUTHOR

Susan Keene was born in California and raised in Illinois. She spent the first fifteen years of her career in the medical profession. She likes to weave her knowledge and experiences into her stories.

Susan is a member of Sleuths-Ink Mystery Writers and Ozarks Romance Authors.

When she is not busy writing, she loves to search for relics with her metal detector, to buy and sell antiques, and is an avid reader.

Keene loves to spend time with her two daughters and three grandchildren.

She lives on a farm in the beautiful Ozarks with her family and her dogs.

Besides her mysteries and crime novels, Susan wrote a children's series featuring her dog, Diggitty.